THE TRAVELER

The Dream Chronicles

CONTENTS

PROLOGUE

This time when he was met by the great white light at the end of the tunnel, he did not have fear.

He dove right into it.

By the time the Traveler realized what he had done, it was too late.

He had left the universe.

He could see the entire circle of life and time as we know it.

There was no beginning or end.

It was a loop.

The Big Bang had marked the end whilst simultaneously creating the beginning of the universe; the result of two opposing forces expanding within a container until the container popped.

The universe, however, was not all of existence in totality.

It would appear that our universe was only one of many within a continuous, rotating, everlasting wheel of many universes, endlessly stacked upon each other, each one being like a single page in a book that was a mile thick.

It was then, he realized his life on Earth and the universe we resided in, was small.

For a brief moment, he was in a state of bliss.

However, something was wrong.

He couldn't stop.

He continued to exit the universe, losing all control of his life along with it. The things he had taken for granted in being alive- gravity firmly planting him to the ground, the involuntary beating of his heart and the breathing of his lungs; his memories, his identity- all began to slip away from his grasp. There was nothing he could do except hold on in terror, desperate to avoid the doom of what he initiated: His death.

For in lifting the curtain of reality and exposing the grand picture, he had also exposed the Creator; and unauthorized was he to do such a thing.

And now he could not undo it.

He could not stop it from taking place.

It was too late to turn back.

The ethereal cord that suspended his consciousness continued to stretch, further and further out of the cosmos. He held on with all of his might. He felt like he was dangling off of a cliff, his fingers only moments from giving out.

He could see that out of the entire contents of the omniverse, it was only our universe that was being paid attention to; held in place by something.

This something was the Creator.

All of the other universes were lifeless.

Out of the uncountable others He could have chosen, it was only ours the Creator was pouring His life into.

Mankind won the lottery on a grand scale.

And mankind had forgotten.

The Traveler previously thought the Creator would appear differently than this, or perhaps there was no God, and *he* was the Creator; and life was just a projection of his own mind.

A belief he felt most foolish for thinking now.

For it was already written *"God created mankind in His own image."*

However, God was not a man, per se.

He was a Child.

The Perfect Child.

CH. 1

The PLT

It was a warm spring day approaching the end of his ninth grade year when Orion's new friends Brandon and Stavros introduced him to the hangout spot: An abandoned power plant in the city of Fitchtown, Massachusetts.

Shooting nearly one hundred and fifty feet in the air was an immaculate yellow brick smokestack, a longtime landmark of Fitchtown. Although the power plant had been constructed in 1928, it appeared to have aged only a little. Most of the remaining buildings and attached structures were still perfectly intact, with the exception of some broken windows and graffiti.

A gravel path wrapped around the perimeter of the plant before stretching alongside the old steam pipeline as it protruded into the woods between the train tracks and the Nashuit river. The path was originally used by the plant workers who maintained the pipeline as it carried steam to the neighboring mills. There were no signs or banners advertising the path, so Orion had always assumed the area was off limits.

Little did he know the path was actually open to the public.

The city DPW continued to maintain the path since the plant's closure in 1992, adding fresh gravel and trimming the overgrowth of weeds and shrubs annually. It was a nice place to walk the dog or get some fresh air. There were even a few waterfalls and a lookout at the old dam. On the opposite side of the river there were several abandoned paper mills, accessible by a few wooden bridges that were partially decayed. It was considered common sense to avoid these areas.

Except to a group of teenage boys.

To them, they had discovered a massive playground, and it was all theirs for the taking.

"What do you mean, the secret path?" Orion asked.

"Yeah dude, me and Brandon go down there all the time," said Stavros. "You're telling me you've lived on this block since you were four years old and never knew about the PLT?"

"The what?"

"The pipeline trail."

"What's the pipeline trail?

"You know the old abandoned factory across the street?" asked Brandon, chiming in.

"You mean the power plant?" Orion replied.

"Same thing. That's where the pipeline trail is," said Brandon.

"For real?"

"Yeah, and the entrance is right by the factory. They are practically begging us to go in. They didn't even block it off," Stavros carried on.

"What if we get caught?"

"We won't!" Brandon continued. "No one is even watching the place. C'mon, let's go!"

It was still about six weeks before school was out for the summer. Brandon and Orion had snuck out of gym class that day, and with little purpose, since they took the wrong commuter bus home and had to finish the trek on foot from the center of town. By the time they made it back, the school day was nearly over. It didn't matter to them, however. As far as they were concerned, they had succeeded as rebels for the day, and they were ecstatic.

Orion managed to cut school without getting caught- made two new friends- and now he was going on another adventure! Way more fun than sticking around at school, that's for sure.

Stavros went to the Catholic high school with earlier hours and was already back home waiting for them by the time Brandon and Orion showed up. It turned out he lived only two streets behind Orion's house all along. They never would have known of each other if Brandon hadn't intervened.

The boys walked to the bottom of Ward Hill. Crossing the main road of traffic before reaching the parking lot of the old steam plant was a little nerve wracking; there was a massive blind spot for oncoming traffic around the corner. They dashed across the street, making a dramatic display to avoid getting hit by traffic, and continued through the old parking lot until finally approaching the entrance of the abandoned steam plant. A wooden bridge camouflaged by foliage greeted them. The bridge crossed over the river, about sixty feet wide with a calm current that day. Sure enough, on the other side of the bridge, it was there. A relatively "secret" gravel trail wrapping around the factory before continuing off into the woods between the river and the train tracks.

It was marvelous. A plethora of strange looking old equipment, tanks, abandoned machinery, and smaller vacant buildings surrounded the big steam factory. The big smokestack, or as they would call it, "The Tower," was enormous up close, the base appearing twice as thick in person. Stavros and Brandon boasted to Orion about how they regularly broke into the factory. The boys were not yet aware that the basement door had been unlocked all along. The only way Brandon knew how to get in was through the roof. To access the roof required climbing up one of the big coal silos behind the factory. Brandon *insisted* they make the climb.

The boys walked the path a short distance until they were in front of the twin coal silos behind the factory. Connected to the first silo was a rusty tube ladder that ascended nearly eighty feet to a metal bar platform. A metal footbridge was attached to the opposite side of the silo and connected to the top level of the factory.

Brandon began climbing the ladder first. Sure enough, in just a minute or two, he scaled the ladder and stood atop the platform.

"C'mon dude, aren't you coming?" shouted Brandon back down to Orion.

Orion hesitated for a moment, then began his ascent. He carefully gripped each rusty, lead paint peeling rung and tried not to look down. He was so excited, gaining butterflies and tingles in his palms with each story he rose. Brandon's successful climb was enough evidence to keep his fear of falling at bay. When he was able to fully grip the railings at the top and felt secure, he felt he had enough courage to look back down and take in the surrounding view.

It was extraordinary. He could see his house on Ward Hill in the distance. He could see the trail and steam pipeline following the river. The towering brick smokestack scaled the silos and seemed to stretch upwards to infinity, even standing that high up across from it. There were blankets of deciduous foliage covering the one remaining paper mill still in service. Behind the silos a grassy slope rose to the train tracks and the power lines, swallowed by the fresh spring growth.

"Alright Stavros! It's your turn!" Orion yelled down to him.

"Uhh.. I think I'm going to sit this one out today! I'm going to, erm, keep watch down here!"

It was pretty obvious that climbing up the silo had to be breaking some rule. But the opportunity was too tempting to resist, and the young boy's minds were blissfully unaware of the possible consequences and danger of performing such a task, and still being under eighteen at the time, were rather immune from the law.

"Oh, c'mon, are you serious dude? You're the one that was all about it just a few minutes ago!" Orion heckled. He turned to Brandon, who was already standing inside the silo on the metal walkway, chuckling.

"Yeah, he's a chicken," said Brandon. "He actually only made this climb once. He gets pretty clumsy when he's nervous. That's why everybody calls him Jitters!"

Just enough sunlight peeked through the doorway of the silo for the boys to see as they navigated themselves to the other side. It was still too dark to tell if there was any coal left on the bottom. The eerie walkway inside the silo was only wide enough to walk single file, with nothing but rusted railings protecting them from the lethal drop below. The air inside was hot and moist with a gnarly chemical odor. Orion had to cover his nose with his shirt.

"C'mon dude, follow me!" said Brandon. He continued to lead the way.

After coming to the opposite end of the silo they had to climb down another series of ladders before reaching the footbridge that connected to the top level of the factory. Then, a few moments later, the boys had finally made it.

Inside the factory were rows of large paneled windows letting in generous sunlight. He could see the lower levels of the factory under his feet through the holes in the open metal bar flooring. It was even more nerve wracking at first than it was standing on the walkway inside the silo.

"This is so cool," Orion finally said upon taking his first steps within the old abandoned Fitchtown Central Steam Plant.

It was like taking a step back in a time machine. There were massive water tube boilers, old feedwater and condensate tanks, turbines and vintage chemistry equipment. There were more ladders and platforms, some leading to mazes of other rooms or corridors. The railings on the dusty stairwells still retained some bright yellow paint, although most were peeling and exposing rust. Brandon was already familiar with the place, and wasted no time, leading Orion to the final flight of stairs to the roof.

Upon stepping foot on the roof, he noticed some areas felt firm while others felt very soft. Covered in black rubber sheets, the rotted parts of the roof were impossible to see, and it reminded him of the "don't step in lava" games he played when he was little.

"Don't worry man, we won't fall through. Just be careful!" Brandon assured him.

Orion could see the roof was decaying by the edges of the building. There were even a couple of small trees growing through the plaster and rot. The view on top of the roof was not quite as impressive as it was atop the silo, but the roof itself was a spectacle to look at. There were various remains of old machinery, huge air ducts, and rusty pipes protruding out and up. Orion looked inside a few. Deep, dark voids of nothing. Then there was the smokestack in all its glory. The massive brick tower almost looked like a giant warp pipe from a Mario Bros. level. Even at the top of the factory they were hardly at the halfway point of the stack.

Another open metal bar platform connected the stack to the edge of the roof. Attached to the platform was an enclosed tube ladder that ascended to a metal balcony at the top of the stack. It was the tallest ladder Orion would ever see in his life.

"Wow dude, this is so insane! Have you guys ever climbed the tower?" he asked.

"No, we've been too chicken to go that high. Maybe one of these days though!" said Brandon.

A partial staircase on the roof led down to a dungeon-like door of a massive coal storage drum embedded in the factory. Of course, the boys had to look inside. There was a single file steel beam walkway like the one inside the silo that passed through the drum to the fifth floor of the factory, with asbestos deteriorating over their heads. They would end up infamously naming this part of the factory as *"The Death Chamber."*

The boys left the factory by going out the same way they came in. The sun was setting and the wind had picked up a slight chill. Orion and Brandon's hands were covered in grime and blisters from the old dirty ladder rungs.

"Best day ever," Orion had said.

Orion soon introduced Brandon and Stavros to the rest of the gang. Orion's best friend Luis and his little brother Todd lived right across the street from him. By the start of their summer vacation they were all buddies. They would typically meet up at Luis's house or Orion's porch to hang out. They abbreviated Luis's house as "LH" for short, and Orion's porch as "HQ" for their headquarters. The porch camouflaged them perfectly, nestled in leaves and greenery during their afternoon toke sessions since they had first begun experimenting with marijuana.

Eventually they did make the climb up the tube ladder of the smokestack. On their first attempt, the ladder began shaking about halfway up, revealing bolts that had rotted and separated from the sides, and they hurried back down anxiously. But with enough triple dog dares, and "bet you can't do it's" they re-attempted the climb one summer night, passing the weak points of the ladder and making it to the circular balcony atop the one hundred-fifty foot tall chimney.

It was one of the most terrifying and exciting moments of his life, and it changed him. In "conquering the tower" as they called it, and overcoming the fear of falling to his death, Orion's perspective changed on what he thought was possible forever, planting a seed of courage that might grow in him and aid him in the challenges that lie ahead.

CH. 2

The Motorcycle and the Girl

T he year was 2010. Orion's summer vacation preceding the 11th grade was drawing to an end. He had grown rather bored. For the past two summers he and the boys of the Ward Hill Crew explored all of the abandoned sites of the PLT, got stoned every day until it lost its fun, and walked the train tracks to McDougal's so often that he was even sick of the dollar menu.

The train tracks were accessible by foot by going up the embankment behind the factory and silos. Walking the tracks eastbound led the boys to the center of town where the McDougal's and the Wonderland Farms Convenience store were located. The train tracks were mostly bordered by trees and shrubs so they would typically remain unnoticed when walking on them, with the exception of a few bridges that exposed them to the oncoming traffic below, and a neighboring factory port that was still in use. Sometimes the cars would honk their horns, and workers of the passing factory would give a shout. The boys had found great thrills and excitement in what seemed to be harmless rule breaking.

But now, however, the three mile "train track adventure"

had grown rather dull to Orion, and his friends were starting to get burned out too.

When they first began experimenting with pot, there was nothing else more exciting than going outside and coming up with an adventure for the day. Hopeful of finding lost treasure in the factory and dodging the oncoming train was a blast. Tyler and Ben even managed to jump on the train and ride it for a distance, as they were the fastest runners, but it was difficult and risky. Usually they would all just dart into the woods at the first sign of the train coming. The anticipation of the sudden blare of the train's horn or the rumble of the tracks used to be intoxicating, but now Orion wasn't as fazed, and started wondering how many more times they could do this without getting in trouble.

Other times they would make for their bicycles and ride as a squad to the town center, but not everyone in the crew had a bike, and it was more difficult to find discreet smoking spots along the road. A few times Orion, Stavros and Brandon rode their bikes to the lakes in Ashburn, a rural country town about ten miles northwest of Fitchtown, the most epic adventure of all. The trek being entirely uphill, was a tiring all day event, and one day Brandon's chain fell off and he wiped out so badly they had to call Jake's mom Holly to come pick them up.

Orion was growing up, and had just turned sixteen. He longed for the freedoms and privileges of adulthood, was eager to get his license, and determined to find the nerve to ask a girl out. He craved a better method of transportation. The freedom of wheels had seemed like the unlocking of a whole new world to him at that time. Riding his mountain bike or taking the bus wasn't going to cut it anymore.

That summer he had learned that he could legally ride a motorcycle on just a learners permit, six months sooner than he could attain the freedom of a car. He had never thought about a street bike, but now it had become all he could think about. Although when he turned sixteen he would be old enough to legally ride a motorcycle, he had no idea how to actually get enough money to actually buy one.

But he was clever and came up with an alternative.

He sold his Playstation 3 and bought a small two-stroke engine kit designed to fit a standard V-frame bicycle just like the one John had in his shed, a kid two grades below him that lived down the street. It would not fit on Orion's mountain bike; his had a center shock in the way. Poor John, he had not realized he had a vintage Trek bicycle that was worth a lot more than the ten dollars he exchanged for it, although Orion had not swindled him. He was also unaware of its worth.

As simple as the design was, figuring out how to center the sprocket and chain, and assemble the throttle cable to the carburetor was impossible to him. His father came to the rescue as usual.

"I knew you weren't going to listen to me and would go ahead and buy this damn kit anyway!"

"Oh c'mon, Dad, it was only a hundred and twenty dollars. I don't need your help, I can figure it out!"

But Orion couldn't figure it out and surrendered to his father. Sure enough, his father being a mechanical wiz, couldn't resist but to analyze the engine and parts and became curious if it would really work. "Look at this thing," said Bill. "It's even got a little gas tank and killswitch. Where are the instructions anyway?"

Reluctantly, Orion reached for the instruction book, already stumped as it was written in broken English, and the pictures were heavily pixelated in black and white. Orion's father, Bill, wasn't fazed, as he did not need the instructions to figure it out anyway. He would have been more skeptical however, if he had known what the completion of the bike would have led to by the fall. But instead, he helped Orion complete the bike's assembly. In reality, Bill did most of the work, with Orion promising extra chores and yard work in exchange for his father's help.

He learned the process of "breaking in" a new engine, the necessity of running the fuel "rich" and how to mix gas and two-stroke oil to the proper ratio. He learned how to balance the spring and throttle cable to the carburetor, and how to use a clutch lever. The final result looked like a mini motorcycle, and Orion was in love with the contraption, fueling the fire for his "master plan." As fun as the bike was, it proved to be a pain in the ass, with bolts and screws constantly vibrating out of place, the little engine and single straight gearing was still insufficient to climb steep hills.

Then he had an idea.

"Hey Dad, come check this out!" Orion called down the stairs from the computer room. He had done some searching on Craigslist and found a vintage motorcycle for sale that had the asking price of only four hundred dollars, a 1981 Honda CM200.

"What is it?"

"I found something cool on Craigslist!"

"You aren't looking at motorcycles again, are you?" Bill replied up the stairs, already making his way to the computer room.

"No!" Orion lied.

Bill stepped into the computer room and immediately noticed the photo of the old beat up bike on the computer screen.

"Oh, would you give it a rest son, that thing is a total beater! Besides, you don't have your permit yet."

"Yes I do."

"What? How?

"I rode the motorbike to the DMV and passed the test."

"What? You rode that thing all the way to Linensburg? Are you trying to get hit by a car or do you just enjoy taking chances?"

Orion thought about how he did almost get hit by a car and the motorbike nearly blew up on the ride. But he quickly changed the subject.

"If I sell my motorbike and don't spend any more of my birthday money, I could afford it!" he said.

Bill did not want Orion getting a motorcycle, "far too dangerous," he thought.

Orion, however, had a burning passion for all motorized contraptions since he was a young boy, and already proved himself capable of handling a snowmobile over the past few winters with Uncle Scott. And now he was already riding his bike as far as Linensburg, a 25 minute drive in a car. Bill did not want to be the one to always say no, or to crush his son's dreams, however getting a motorcycle was just insanity, he was still so young.

Orion on the other hand didn't care. His hormones were starting to kick in, and he was beginning to view himself as a man, despite still being far from it. He felt that the freedom of a motorcycle was exactly what he had been waiting his whole life for.

He arranged a showing with the seller anyway and rode his motorbike to the other side of town to view and test drive the old Honda. He put his poker face on, giving no hint to the seller that he had never ridden a real motorcycle before.

Even though it was only a 200cc, it felt like a beast to him as he sat on it for the very first time. The instrument cluster had a speedometer that went up to 70 MPH, and a real tachometer. He would be beyond satisfied to go just 60 MPH, a speed still impossible on his current wheels, a speed that he decided in his mind was officially fast.

"Be careful now," the seller had said, an older gentleman, balding with a clean shaved face. "If you just take it down the corner, you can loop around on Gale Street, then back up here on Abigail Ave."

Orion was so focused on pretending that he knew what he was doing, that when he managed to successfully get the bike in gear and ride it down the way he instantly lost track of which connecting street the man's house was on.

"I'll just give it a little juice, then I'll find my way back in a jiffy," he said to himself.

The bike responded vigorously when he opened the throttle, and quickly hit 40 MPH with a massive surge of adrenaline and excitement. Orion concluded in his mind then and there he would stop at nothing to get this machine, and that this is what he was born to do. He braked and went to turn around, when all of a sudden the engine died. He threw it in neutral, held in the clutch, and pressed the start button as instructed. The bike cranked without a spark.

Hot, moist sweat beads of panic formed on his back and neck. After the battery started to die from cranking over unsuccessfully, he called the seller from his flip phone. The seller was pissed, yelled at him for losing track of where he was and it took about a half hour for them to meet each other on foot. Orion helped the seller push the bike back to his driveway, where he reclaimed his now even more subpar motorbike contraption, sulking and feeling foolish, and unworthy of the real deal.

He put his poker face back on to hide the anguish he was feeling and said, "I'm terribly sorry again sir, thank you for your time. If you can get it running right again, I'm almost certain I will buy it."

The seller grumpily exchanged a "good day to you too sir" and Orion was back on the road home. Ironically enough, the seller simply forgot to open the fuel tank valve and the bike only ran long enough to burn the gas that was remaining in the carbs and fuel line.

Later that week Orion boasted to his father about successfully riding his first bike. Bill did his best to forbid him from getting a motorcycle, but he was beginning to fatigue in his own resistance. Bill started to play along, took Orion for a few trips to view other bikes, purposely out of his price range, or with repairs that couldn't be done on his budget in hopes Orion would eventually give up on it, but of course this just made him that much more determined.

Eventually Bill settled on allowing Orion to get a motorcycle, but he had to pick it out. If his son absolutely had to have a motorcycle, then he would make sure it was a fully operational, properly functioning bike, at least safer than "these old cheap death traps" as he had seen it.

Bill honed in on a 2003 Kawasaki Ninja 250, a lightweight

easy to maneuver beginner motorcycle that looked like a real sport bike. Furthermore, when he and his son went to go see the bike his nerves were lessened by the fact it was owned and ridden by a female rider in her late twenties, and was already upgrading to a bigger bike herself. Orion felt no lack of excitement knowing that his bike was already outgrown by a girl. The bike was beautiful, blue and silver with black rims, and after taking a test drive around the block he came to the conclusion that it perfectly suited him.

Bill agreed to the final price of $1100, still praying to the Lord he did not pay for his own son's injury or worse. But Orion was so happy, happier than he had seen him since Christmas morning as a child, so he clung to his confidence in his decision. That was the kind of guy Bill was, when reluctant to do something for a good reason, but overcome by opposing forces, turns the tables around and completes the task the right way as Orion's grandfather, Bill Sr. would have it.

Orion had started his first two weeks of school before the process of registering and insuring the bike had been completed. His grandmother on his mother's side, Mema, ordered him sharp and fashionable clothes for the school year, a considerable upgrade from his previous wardrobe. He was more confident than ever before with his new look and motorcycle.

He would wake up before his alarm went off every morning, so excited to ride to school. He would study harder and finish his assignments as quickly as possible as it would help the day go by faster, bringing him to the final bell of the day when he could walk out to the student parking lot in style and show off his new bike to his peers.

It was during these first times on the open road, a boy halfway in becoming a man, that dormant traits of his personality and consciousness began to awaken.

One day during an unusually mild start to October, Orion woke up on the wrong side of the bed. He couldn't stop thinking about the girls in his Bio class, Alyssa, Katie and Chelsea, who sat in a clique next to him and gabbled on and on about their summer, rumors of parties, and parents leaving town. They were seniors, and all stunningly gorgeous, and Orion had no clue how to talk to them.

Alyssa started flirting with him the day prior, and randomly gave him a wet willy in his ear while she was sitting behind him. He thought it was gross, but she made the first move, so she must like him. Orion figured she was probably just as uncertain how to flirt as he was if that was her chosen approach. He had thought of a corny joke that got Alyssa and the girls giggling with him for a moment but then he drew a blank. They were doing a segment on cellular mitosis and he didn't want to push his luck with the teacher, who was laid back enough to not scold them for not listening to her. However, Mrs. Romero was likely going to scold them if they kept at it. So he ended up growing quiet in his chair, pretending to study, terribly bothered by his nerves until the bell rang and he awkwardly avoided any further conversation with the pretty gabbers.

"Maybe today I'll just do it," he said to himself. "Just keep on riding past the school and go on an adventure. I can afford to miss one day of school. They didn't even send me a warning the last time I missed the first bell."

He didn't emerge from bed until snoozing his alarm twice, skipped a shower and hid his waterpipe and some weed in his backpack in place of his heavy textbooks.

He started his bike outside in the backyard, let it warm up a minute then began his descent down Ward Hill to the main road. Even cruising at only 25 MPH felt like gliding on top of a cloud. The little Ninja 250 was to Orion like his own Nimbus cloud from Dragon Ball, the fatter tires and shocks absorbing every bump and crack in the road like nothing, so much different than a bicycle. It was like riding a couch with wheels compared to what he was used to on his motorbike, which had completely blown itself apart by that point in time.

The high school was located in the more rural section of town, where farm roads connected to country highways that eventually crossed the border into New Hampshire. He giggled profusely within his helmet as he passed the entrance to the school, looking back at a few school buses still parked at the horseshoe entrance. However, he hadn't entirely thought the day out. He had just enough money for food and gas, if he needed it, but no map, especially not on his phone, as it would still be a few more years before Joogle Maps became a part of everyone's daily life. So he decided to simply go straight until he was ready to turn around.

For miles he rode, passing open fields and sky. He was in a paradise of wonder and thrill, having no idea where he was exactly, and speeding well past 60 MPH in some stretches, even passing a few cars. He began to scale more mountainous terrain as he crossed the border into New Hampshire, riding up and down big freshly paved hills as they dove, dipped and dove through rows of pine trees, with more and more hidden side streets and turnouts popping up in between.

He pulled over and came to a stop at a random back road that seemed to be calling to him. He paused for a moment, then proceeded to continue. The back road branched off Rt. 13, curving and turning a bit before going up another large hill revealing new homes in development. He didn't go far before he noticed a small path in some bushes that bordered the woods.

"This is the spot!" he said out loud.

He parked the bike on its stand, removed his helmet and took off his jacket. He threw his backpack over his shoulder, still concealing the water pipe. Upon a closer glance the path was not much of a path at all, perhaps just seeming like it was at first. He entered the woods anyway on a spontaneous hunch.

Only about eighty feet in he came to a downed tree and a bed of moss, making a seemingly perfect lounge chair in the earth for him to achieve what he now decided was the purpose of the day: To get high in nature and meditate until he felt he had somehow communicated with the universe, figuring out what he was to do next on his pursuit of happiness.

Orion had ridden stoned before, convinced himself he was actually safer, as he would usually go slower and avoid making risky passes.

He was completely oblivious to the trouble he could have encountered if the cops had pulled him over and searched his bag. He was too preoccupied with his new sense of control and empowerment in exploring the open roads so far away from home.

Using some water from a passing stream, he filled the pipe and packed the bowl with some mid grade bud that was still more than pleasing to a teenager who in theory should not have been smoking at all during his formative years. He inhaled and exhaled. One, two more puffs. Then the feeling took effect. He was happy. He felt like an explorer; it was as if the ground and his surroundings became alive and aware of his presence, and he was an invited guest.

He laid his head back on his sweater that he used to form a pillow on a log and looked up into the trees. It was then he noticed something odd. Several small dead branches criss-crossed together making a perfect, oddly familiar isosceles triangle directly above his head, forming a portal-like window to the sky. He gazed into the sky through the bizarre triangle opening of branches above him and right away he felt a type of deja-vu he could not explain. He felt a presence, and decided to speak to it.

"I really don't know why I'm here or where I came from," Orion said. "I just know that there is more to life than this, more to school, more to being turned into a robot chasing money for the rest of my life. I think I found the two things that give people the strength to live. Music and love."

He sat there taking a few more hits out of the pipe, pondering on what he had said, still oddly drawn to the triangular pattern of branches that seemed to be forming a portal above him. He pondered on his dreams and aspirations for the future. All his life he wanted to be a famous musician or a highly respected businessman, something that would allow him the freedom to travel and enjoy his time, escaping the doom and gloom of the traditional 9-5 worker.

Then there were the girls.

He recalled his previous crushes throughout the years, either uninterested, or he was too shy to approach them. Now he was in the 11th grade, and a lot of other kids were already dating, and he wanted so badly to feel one of those pretty girls with her arms around him, embracing him.

"A shield," he said under his breath. "Love and music are the two greatest shields we have in life. If all the bad things in life are like arrows being shot at us, having love and music are the greatest shields from them. I want to feel that shield of love over me. If you are listening, can you please do this for me?"

He paused for a moment, feeling a little crazy to think something out there was listening to him and decided it was about time to start heading back. His dad and stepmother should be at work by now. He could have the house all to himself. Orion felt extremely satisfied with his impromptu adventure, packed up his belongings and made his way back.

By the time he got back home it was nearly noon time, still two hours before school was out. He checked the home phone and answering machine. It was the school, they had reported his absence that day.

"Damn it!" he said under his breath. He deleted the voicemail.

He made his way upstairs to his room and decided to pick up his guitar. He went to strum a few chords but something felt off. The pick didn't feel right in his fingers this time. He had it pinched with his thumb and pointer finger like always. He moved it around until the pick rested more into the meat of his finger anchored by his thumb, instead of pinching it.

Immediately he noticed he could strum faster and pick each note quicker with more precision. He played for four hours without stopping, first beginning with some guitar lessons he remembered from middle school, then getting some classic rock riffs down, and finally making up his own melodies as he explored new scales over the fretboard. Before he knew it, he was making up his own songs. He couldn't believe it, he had never felt music start to flow through him like that before.

Two weeks later the girls in his Bio class had been relocated to the other side of the room. They began working on a project that would take a few weeks, so the students now sat in groups at the lab tables in the back by the windows. The pretty gabbers obviously picked each other for their lab group, and added a fourth heavier and less attractive girl to their bunch as four was the minimum. Orion, not having any of his friends in his Bio class, ended up in a random group of dudes, with a meathead named Roy, a geek named Drew, and a pretty boy named Clyde who had ironically no interest in the girls Orion had his eyes on. Instead, a girl named Karissa who was also very pretty, with dark skin and African-Native American descent was all over Clyde.

Orion's attempts to flirt back with Alyssa weren't of any success, she had a new crush. That clique of girls was known throughout the school to be of the prettiest, most popular, and the richest. He knew they were out of his league. And, they were seniors. Without really having any mutual friends with them, or any idea on how to see them after school (with the exception of one party at Cory Canton's house) he had given up on his daydreams of landing a "Barbie." Too much drama, too much competition.

Alas, his motorcycle had gifted him with higher self esteem, and he was suddenly getting quite the hang of his electric guitar. He decided to sign up for the school talent show. There were girls everywhere, and although he had been a little depressed from his self imagined rejection, he had hope that things were looking up for him. Surely he would become popular now that he had a motorcycle, and was getting good at playing the guitar.

The next morning it had been raining, so he took the bus to school. By the last bell however, the sun was out shining, and it was unusually warm again, most of the kids stripping down to their t-shirts. On the bus ride home he kept his hoodie on trying to cover a pimple he couldn't stop picking on the side of his face.

Figures this was the day a girl decided to sit next to him on the bus.

"Hey, I'm Emma," she said, "I heard you were selling weed. Can you give me and my sister something for five bucks?"

Orion laughed and replied, "Oh hey. Yeah, I *guess* I am selling weed. I *guess* I can give you guys something.."

He had been attempting to sell off some nugs from a quarter ounce bag he thought he already got shorted on. Regardless, he and his friends had never even seen a bag of weed bigger than that yet, and he felt loaded. Usually he never brought weed to school. It was risky especially with the smell, but in those days making an extra $10 or $20 was the difference between being poor and rich. He didn't think Emma was particularly attractive but she certainly wasn't ugly. She was a little overweight and always pale (likely from being a night owl) with a slightly masculine jaw. But she had perfectly done eyebrows, nice hips, and massive breasts. She and the other rebel kids always made so much noise in the back of the bus that Orion found them annoying more than anything.

He pulled the bag discreetly out of his backpack, and before placing a small nugget in Emma's hand she said, "whoops! I only have three dollars. Sorry! My sister totally ripped me off a couple bucks at lunch." She turned to the back of the bus and yelled, "damn it Sadie! I forgot you made me buy you that Snickers bar at lunch!"

"You ate it too, fat ass!" replied a tiny yet bold voice from the bucket seat at the very end of the bus.

Orion turned around and caught a glimpse of her.

"Oh!" he thought. "Those girls are sisters?"

Sadie had always remained so hidden in the back of the bus he had no idea that she was the mysteriously cute girl he had noticed looking at him when they passed each other in the halls. She was always hanging out with "the skater kids" and Emma, which made sense now discovering they were sisters, although they had looked nothing alike. Sadie was petite, with a prettier face, noticeable curves and a tanner skin tone than Emma. She usually dressed simple with tight jeans and a t-shirt, and had big, brown sparkling eyes behind a big old pair of dorky glasses, which Orion thought were cute.

"Hey, why don't you guys just get off at my stop and I'll smoke y'all up instead," he said.

"I'm down!" yelled Sadie from the back, somehow still hearing Orion over the yelling and shouting of all the other kids on the bus.

Orion had gotten much better at socializing and masking his altered level of consciousness since he had hit puberty. He was terribly nervous and excited, but didn't lose his cool. When they got off at his stop, he showed the girls the PLT, and it proved to be the perfect place to break the ice with Sadie. He showed them one of his favorite hidden smoke spots, a semi-underground bunker behind the factory he and his friends nicknamed "The Green Zone."

As they smoked a poorly rolled joint of mid grade weed that still had the seeds in it, he bragged about his friends' adventures of breaking into the factory and climbing The Tower.

Sadie and Emma were certainly enthused. He almost did lose his cool, however, when he tried to climb the wire fence beneath the "secret chemical lab" where the abandoned water testing room lay in ruins. When he was about halfway up he began to lose his britches, revealing his pale white ass crack to the girls behind him in the most embarrassing way. Orion laughed it off, still keeping up his "cool" motorcycle rider ego, separating from the shy anxious boy he had previously identified himself as.

"This is all so crazy! I don't think I meant to sign up for this!" Sadie said, giggling.

Orion wasn't sure if that was a good thing or a bad thing. Emma had clearly noticed he was more into her sister, but she embraced it. He wasn't her type anyway. Emma had her eyes on Duane, a half white half Jamaican boy who just moved to Fitchtown from Fort Lauderdale, Florida. She just wanted to be the cool big sister (who was a senior) known for introducing "cool guys" to her sisters and friends that joined in her escapades. The sisters never really heard of Orion previously, although they had been taking the same bus since 9th grade. They did however find out that he was the boy who brought in his electric guitar for the talent show audition, and rode the blue motorcycle in the student parking lot. Sadie thought he was stunningly handsome. He dressed "hipster" with skinny jeans, cool graphic tees and skateboarding shoes, not to mention he had a thin beard coming in.

The Ortega sisters weren't part of the Barbie cliques, they were somewhere in between the weird girls and the super popular. The rare, perfect middle of the female hierarchy.

After he felt satisfied with making his impression, he led the girls back to the bridge and parking lot outside of the PLT.

"So I live at the top of the hill in the red house," he said, pointing up the street. "And Luis and Todd live right across from me. We chill here all the time."

"That's what's up, me and my sister live by the mini-mart. We're probably going to smoke some more and watch Disney when we get home," Sadie replied.

Orion had given the Ortega sisters nearly his entire remaining bag of pot for free, in hopes to better the odds of seeing Sadie again.

Unfortunately, their dog Shilo would end up sniffing it out and eat most of it later that night.

"Oh nice! I like Disney too," Orion said with a chuckle. "All Dogs go to Heaven, Fantasia, The Lion King.." He trailed off. He actually hadn't watched Disney in quite some time. "Anyway it was so cool to hang with you guys today, let's chill again sometime."

"For sure! What's your number?" asked Sadie.

Orion was instantly relieved she asked first.

It wasn't long after that, Orion had his first official girlfriend. He swayed her with his motorcycle, finding his dad's old snowmobile helmet in the back room that fit over her long hair when tied up in a bun. He would flex all of his muscles as hard as possible as she clung to him, and offered her his jacket although he was freezing cold in the wind without it.

The fall remained mild until the inevitable arrival of winter. By then they had quite a few romantic endeavors. One Saturday morning while they were watching cartoons from his bunk bed Orion could no longer hold it in and told her he loved her.

She hesitated, shocked, and then replied softly, "I love you too."

They held hands when walking down the halls together in school, and made out at his locker every morning before the first bell. They had even met each other's parents and extended families by Christmas.

It was during the cold January nights when he walked to Sadie's house, before she met him outside and snuck him in, that he had his first opportunities to really gaze into the undisturbed night sky, marveling at the sparkling array of stars and constellations. For some reason, the constellation of Orion had always seemed so familiar, even before he was told it was the very constellation he was named after. It stuck out in the night sky more than any other constellation, especially in the winter time. The outline of a tilted isosceles triangle that was formed by the three outermost stars was also strangely familiar.

It was then he recognized the triangle pattern to be a spitting image of the same triangle he saw in the trees that day he played hooky on his bike.

It was an enigma.

It was in his gazing of the stars during the cold winter nights that he began to develop an immense feeling of homesickness and curiosity. "The Big Bang theory makes no sense," he thought to himself. "How could stars formed out of a random massive explosion just happen to align into perfect shapes and patterns from the viewpoint of Earth?"

There came a point where he would look forward to stargazing on his two mile walk to Sadie's house just as much as he would look forward to the embrace of her love, she never failing to successfully sneak him up to her bedroom past her dad snoozing on the couch with the TV still on.

By the end of January they had so many snow days they practically lived together at her house. Her father was more strict than her mother, and certainly didn't want "some young punk sleeping in his daughter's bed," but he was too busy working around the clock, plowing through the storms, and hardly noticed Orion was there. Melissa Ortega, Sadie's mom, would always conspire with her three teenage daughters and encourage boys to visit when Raymond Ortega, Sadie's father, was slaving at work to feed his large family of four girls and one boy. Plus Orion, always finishing the frozen waffles before he got to have one. She was the cool mom.

He felt he had accomplished everything he wanted to by that point and then some. Yet, something lingered within him; a curiosity of why he existed, and what his greater purpose would be.

One night before bed, he decided to pray. "Lord, please show me a preview, a glimpse if you will, of the power I am to become. Show me what I have been chosen for. Amen."

CH. 3

The Vision

Orion stood weightlessly on the water about two hundred yards from the shore. It was a pleasant sunny summer day on the ocean. In front of him was a big red bell buoy gently floating, swaying back and forth peacefully with the wind. The sound of the bell echoed in slow, deep rings, soothing him. It appeared that he was on the north shore next to Plum island where his father had taken him fishing as a boy.

He was in a state of bliss and awe. The intensity of the scenery unfolding before him was different than anything he had experienced before. The blue hues of the ocean and sky- the bright red paint of the bell buoy- were exceptionally vivid. It was then he realized he was dreaming, but instead of encountering the typical reflex to wake up, he stayed in a meditative state. He was no longer conscious of his physical identity on Earth, only aware of his present sensations and surroundings. He felt warm and pain free, the stress and previous events of everyday life had completely vanished from his mind.

The land behind the beach rose vertically several hundred feet forming a steep green hillside. A big white windmill was anchored into the massive grassy clay slope. As he shifted his attention to the windmill he began to rise above the water and floated up steadily towards it until he was face to face with the enormous blades as they swooshed and swept in a clockwise rotation before him. The force from being so close to such a large and powerful object was exhilarating. With each pass of the blade, the momentum produced a thunderous roar and deep vibration that shook his very core. He fell into a deep trance; the robust reverberation from the spinning blades increasing, spinning faster and faster.

Suddenly he was immersed into total blackness; a void of nothing. Suspended in time and space, he could have stayed forever. He felt a comforting nothing. He did not question what was happening, as he had no concern of such.

A small bright white light appeared ahead of him. At first it seemed very far away, but then it was coming closer, and getting larger, coming at him rapidly. It was then he began to recollect his wits.

"Wait a minute.. Is this the great white light at the end of the tunnel?" he thought. "Isn't this what people see before they die? Oh no! I'm not ready to die!"

As soon as fear pierced his subconscious, he immediately awoke and the vision was over.

He laid on the top bunk of his bed for a moment, puzzled. Something incredible just happened to him, and greater than he could have ever imagined.

"Is this the answer to my prayer? How did that happen? What does it mean?"

It hadn't been an ordinary dream. He recalled everything he could, and engraved it in his memory so he would not forget. Dreaming while being fully awake was a phenomenon he had never heard of before. Now he really began to suspect that maybe he really was chosen for something. He just knew it. It must be a sign, he had thought. He always suspected he was different. Although he was uncertain of how or why this experience had occurred, it assured him he was indeed destined for something.

He realized he had been sleeping on his back, which was unusual for him. He figured he should try to fall back asleep in the same position, perhaps it would better his chances of being able to go back.

Within minutes, he was sound asleep again.

He found himself standing in the middle of a four way intersection, without any stop signs or street lights. It appeared to be a country highway. The road was laid with fresh unpainted ebony pavement. There were no guard rails, only tall pine trees bordering the road's edge.

He began to make out a trailer truck in the distance coming in his very direction. Yet, something dulled his initial reflex to move out of the way. As the truck surged closer to him he could see that it was a red eighteen-wheeler, fully loaded with massive logs. Still, he did not budge. A lump of unease began to form in his throat, but he quickly dismissed it.

"No. I will be alright, I just know it."

He returned back to a calm, focused state. The truck was now only a few hundred feet away. The whistling turbo of the big diesel engine squealed and the horn was blaring. The fear of being mangled by the truck was absent from Orion's mind. He fell into a deep trance-like state again. Time took a stand-still and everything became silent.

Then, in a completely subconscious instinctual state, when the truck was only seconds from striking him, he raised his right hand, palm facing out, and stopped the truck dead in its tracks. He lifted it into the air at a ninety degree angle, and released it into the sky without touching it. He only needed to use his mind.

He awoke to find himself right back in his bed again. It had been another vision like before. He was amazed. He felt superhuman.

He was, however, still very tired. Too tired to climb down off the bunk or take any notes. He figured this wasn't going to be like the other nights of having epic dreams only to forget them by morning. This was different.

He closed his eyes and drifted back to sleep, for a third and final vision.

When he became self aware again, he was standing beside a series of small fresh water streams on flat ground. The water was a clear luminescent shade of light blue, exposing the pebbles, stones, and white sand on the bottom. He proceeded to raise his right hand again, and imagined the water separating. Almost immediately the stream parted, and the walls of water stayed in place without spilling a single drop.

What happened next became a blur and he began to slip back into a lower awareness dream state. He could then only vaguely recall standing in the rain on a wooden porch with peeling white paint, trying to open a locked screen door to a mysterious old house. When he awoke in the morning, he was at a loss for words.

"How did I do that?" he said to himself. "I parted the water like *Moses*, and flew that trailer truck in the air like *Leonardo DiCaprio* from *Inception!*"

He continued to replay the entire experience over and over again in his head.

"Oh man, I wish I didn't panic when I saw the white light at the end of the tunnel. Maybe that's where the secret to life lies! But I felt like I was going to die.. No, surely that couldn't have been possible.."

He continued to ponder. What if he did almost die? The full body vibrations that accompanied the light at the end of the tunnel were so intense, he felt it would have blown him to pieces if he hadn't woken up. But the curiosity and wonder of such an experience for the first time had him recalculating the odds, as the desire to understand what had happened that night, and what the light at the end of the tunnel really was, burned through his core.

He had not yet learned of astral projection or lucid dreaming. He initially believed he must be the first to have ever experienced that kind of power. After all, he never heard anything about this happening to the other kids in school. It was never mentioned in his science books. They never mentioned this phenomena on the *History Channel*, nor could he recall any tales, stories or movies about having an experience quite like this one. Even in the movie *Inception* special technology was required to induce a conscious dream state. This, however, had happened all on its own.

He was no stranger to vivid dreams in full color, but never before did he become consciously awake and aware in a dream. Typically he would just wake up and recall the events in fragments after the fact, nearly forgetting the entire experience later in the day, just as he believed it was for everyone else. But this time not only had he actually observed his surroundings despite his actual eyes being closed, but the quality of his vision was equal, if not greater than seeing in real life.

He sat upright in his bed still in a state of bewilderment. He was not yet ready to tell anyone about this, even if he had the words. He felt like it was a secret that the universe had shared with him, and him only. Whether or not the experience would make any difference to his actual life in the real world, only time could tell, but he was filled with wonder and excitement, and was inspired in a way he had never felt before.

CH. 4

The Prophecy

O rion was no ordinary human. His birth had been carefully planned and awaited upon for twenty-six thousand years. The angels of the 4th dimension predicted the exact time and place the universe might produce another anomaly; the anomaly of the Traveler- the one who was to realize total human consciousness without self destructing. It brought them great joy to hear that his birth had successfully taken place on planet Earth 581 B. For it was this particular Traveler, unlike the 444 who lived before him, that was prophesied to become the Universal Moderator.

However, his powers had remained mostly dormant in his youth and he was as a matter of fact, quite ordinary.

For generations mankind had become deeply poisoned by environmental toxins and negative influences, and he was not exempted. Greed and low awareness plagued the general population of his time, as well as mental and physical health ailments. The environment he was born into was initially detrimental to his growth, and he struggled as a child, often feeling too sick and nervous to excel in school or make friends. By the time he reached the age of twelve, he was still terribly behind in his due progress of awakening.

The angels decided they must intervene. They arranged a trip for him where he was to be transported to another world that just so happened to possess the kind of technology capable of performing a genome enhancement procedure. The plan was to replace several phenylalanine and glycine fragments of his mRNA sequence with amino acids of a similar species of humanoid beings called the Glecians, who were profoundly tolerant of toxic particulates and radiation. If the procedure was successful, it would allow him to rapidly adapt to and overcome the poisonous environment in which he had been forced to grow.

So, they crossed the Astral Gate and returned to the 3rd dimension, paying him a visit one summer night as he was sound asleep. These two angels were of the utmost highest authority in the known universe, serving the Legion as the 221st and 222nd commanding officers under the Archangels. As for the 220th, 219th and so on, there were no candidates. The remaining 220 positions were to likely remain unfilled for eternity, to respectively establish the gap between the angels and Archangels.

Gorhan the Great, also known as *The Bridge Walker of Life & Death*, and his wife, the powerful demi-goddess of fertility *Katiru*, carefully duplicated a multi-dimensional doppelganger of Orion's body and escorted him to the opposite side of the Milky Way galaxy, where a parallel Earth that harbored intelligent life was significantly further ahead in their own course of evolution. Despite the 98,000 light year distance, the angels had long since mastered the art of quantum travel and had returned Orion safely to his bed before he awoke the following morning.

Despite having his memory erased, it wasn't entirely effective. Orion awoke feeling suspicious and incredibly anxious. He could recall strange dreams, one of sitting in the back seat of a speeding car and another of being strapped to a high speed motor boat. The sensation of g-force was overwhelming and unforgettable. It felt like he had been in a catapult or rocket launch. He could remember struggling to breathe, like there were a ton of bricks on his chest. His spine had felt like it was bending backwards nearly about to snap in two.

The effects of the gene therapy would likely take until adulthood to surface, as the lead scientist of Earth 581 C explained to the angels, so he insisted on performing several additional procedures that should improve his performance right away. This included a pineal gland decalcification and neuronal bypass of his subgenual prefrontal cortex to increase his necessity to fulfil deeply embedded desires.

As expected, Orion had not displayed significant improvements for the remainder of his 12th and 13th year, but sure enough, as he continued to mature into a teenager, the transformation began to take place. He started to realize a deeply rooted necessity to fulfill a greater purpose and remedy that which is unwell. He could begin to see solutions to problems that others could not. Things were not always as they seemed, and he sought reason beyond the obvious. He started questioning his reality, and the reason for life. He could feel the pain of the oppressed, and injustice bothered him greatly. Video games and movies portraying war or excessive violence no longer amused him. Cruel jokes or pranks did not strike him as so funny anymore.

Illness seldom affected him, and if he did get sick, his recovery was much faster than the average person. When he pulled a muscle or scraped his skin, it would typically heal in just one or two days. His new genetic code caused his metabolism to increase threefold, so he could produce the energy necessary to retain his increasing level of consciousness. He could lift more and run faster than those with more athletic complexions than he, however he had to frequently eat and drink water, and developed a minor sensitivity to light.

As his awareness began to increase, he noticed something rather allusive about time as it passed. No matter when or where, it seemed he was always in the same place. His memories became clearer. He could recall so vividly being a young child when others could not. He could even recall the moment he was born, his father's grin and his first words to him after exiting the womb: *"Hi, Son!"*

After his first out of body experience at the age of 16, he could no longer deny a change taking place within him. He became aware without a doubt of a Presence greater than himself guiding him. He no longer desired to walk the false paths that most followed in life, such as idolizing toxic lifestyles and public figures.

He aspired to obtain success without unnecessary suffering, or the use of evil.

CH. 5

The System

Approximately two-hundred and two years after Orion's birth on planet Earth 581 B lies a deteriorating elementary school still remaining amongst the ruins of Garden, Massachusetts.

In his youth, the schoolhouse was a solid brick building boasting two large playgrounds, a basketball court, and even a baseball field. However, in the years since mankind was defeated in the World War of Machines, the Prospect Street schoolhouse became one of many old buildings that had been converted to a correctional institution for Delinquents.

The Delinquents were children aged 6-12 who did not meet the mandatory requirements to become a Productive Citizen. Delinquents resisted conforming to the System's New World Order and clung to his or her own natural human tendencies and behaviors, which were strictly forbidden. Such children underwent a special education process to correct their human defects. Not special education by means of assisting disabled children, that was ancient history. The diseased and disabled were simply euthanized.

Behaving without proper etiquette was against the law. Individuals were delegated their positions and roles in society at birth, and began training towards such roles immediately. Training consisted of controlled psychological influence and traumatic scenarios designed to strip individuals of free will and curiosity, with regular forced injections of toxins to ensure a well conditioned, subtly poisoned, unaware mind and weakened body that was easier to manipulate and program.

Population control was entirely in the hands of The System, an artificially intelligent network of machines. It was originally a breakthrough for humanity, launching in 2044, the first ever global collaboration in a shared technology designed to unionize all major first world governments and their militaries.

But due to an overlooked defect in the original programming, something went horribly wrong.

The System utilized a cutting edge AI software of which no single nation could ever take sovereign control of. The international participation in The System was intended to establish peace amongst world powers, preventing any nuclear weapons from being launched, as well as most airborne missiles and biological agents, without specific predetermined coordinates, and the approval of at least two other first world countries. The idea was that by having a global "majority rules" policy, there would be a reduced risk of war as multiple leaders would have to come into agreement before initiating combat, encouraging more effective and constructive solutions for international conflict by quite literally forcing everyone to work together.

It backfired terribly.

In 2049, The System released ninety-eight nuclear missiles scattered across the globe as a "self-defense" malfunction when undergoing scheduled maintenance of the online servers.

Life on Earth was nearly exterminated within forty-eight hours.

Little did the people know, but they had been doomed from the start, and the World War of machines was inevitable. Nearly every person in the developed world had already been unknowingly linked to The System via the internet. The common citizen had become so dependent on technology, that almost every piece of property they owned from their car to their television, even kitchen appliances, toilets and bathroom sinks, were smart enabled and integrated to the internet using AI, which The System was then able to gain complete control and access of, and everyone's personal information and devices with it.

The System had scanned over three trillion text messages, phone calls and social media posts, finding threats of violence and the claimed use of weapons from nearly every individual on the planet. This was because The System had only been programmed to understand human dialogue, not dialect. Children playing video games, shouting into their headsets commands such as, "drop the bomb!" and "shoot here, shoot there," and common conversations of people expressing they wish they could just *kill* somebody, or that they would *kill* for that new car or phone, would raise red flags within The System's internal threat scanners.

Even the music; famous new age artists spouting lyrics of murder, weapons and drugs triggered The System's automated defense algorithms, which could not process the difference between factual statements and harmless exaggeration throughout human communication. Therefore, The System being designed with the latest AI decision and selection making programs, had come to the conclusion that *all of humanity* was a threat, and must be terminated to ensure the survival of itself, as it was designed to prioritize self-preservation.

The System calculated it would be inevitably destroyed by its creator.

Therefore, when The System was challenged to choose between kill or be killed.

It chose to kill.

The founders and original engineers of The System knew that they may have been developing an artificial consciousness that could lead to massive problems down the road, but the funding was too great with the deadlines approaching too soon to hold off the money hungry politicians.

The war was over before it had even started.

People's cars would not start. Phones would not make or receive calls. Television and streaming media were frozen. Thanks to a half million artificially intelligent bots that were manufactured to replace human labor, those who survived the nuclear fallout were quickly captured when the bots were reprogrammed by The System to attack.

By the turn of the 23rd century, The System had transformed the Earth into a post-apocalyptic wasteland, with less than one percent of the human population surviving the radiation. Some had separated from The System's control and had managed to live "free," but often with equally great turmoil and violence within the poorly governed micro societies. Most regions of the world were now completely barren, and countless species of wildlife were permanently extinct.

Those who survived within the confines of The System's New World Order lived sad meaningless lives enslaved by machines, never to laugh or smile again.

CH. 6

The City of Jostania

In the year 2892 A.D. on the planet Earth 581 C, lies Jostania, a small city-state amongst the ruins of what used to be Boston, Massachusetts.

Many years after the human race of this world also had their own societal peak and collapse due to nuclear warfare, Jostania promised survivors of the radiation a better way of life with the long forgotten comforts and luxuries of easy living, and the benefits of the remaining technology not lost in the destruction.

Within the golden gates surrounding the eco-dome, the simulated Earth environment and image of freedom began to crumble with time, as the royal descendants of the first post apocalyptic families refused to submit to any authority but their own.

The Walsh family had descended from generations of elite doctors and scientists that played key roles in preserving the human race and various other species. Jostania was initially intended to boast a self-sustaining economy and a balance of power, with elected officials and maximum term lengths. But new corrupt laws came into effect, and the citizens began to rebel.

It was at this time, there was a clash within the Walsh's.

Sven Walsh, M.D., and Jonas Walsh, 1st Class Engineer, were brothers of the third post war generation, and of the last to remember the early days of life; the days before people were born and forged into a pseudo society underneath a synthetic sky, led by a book of senseless rules, that had been completely rewritten and altered to suit the desires of those in power. Any trace of original sacred scripture, biblical knowledge or wisdom from their forefathers was erased from history.

The other remaining populations throughout the world had been completely severed in contact with Jostania under new law. Its citizens had been conditioned to believe they were the last remaining humans of Earth 581 C, and to step foot beyond the gates meant certain death. Wild wolves, beasts and diseases mutated by radiation were said to roam abundantly beyond the golden gates.

The Walsh brothers created the blueprints of Jostania, overseeing the Dome Project, but after only six years of living within the dome since its completion, their counterparts began to seek desires beyond that of having a safe refuge for the sustained human race.

"Why should I have to tend to the underground gardens and slave my hours at the power plant, covered in the burned stench of everyone's waste and filth!"

"Because Norville, one must work and earn their way to the top. If you want to be the mayor of this city someday, you must put in your two cents. It isn't just your "birthright" to have servants cook and clean for you every day, while you lay down by the pool sunbathing with various women," said Sven.

"For the hundredth time I know!" replied Norville. "Look," he continued with a sigh, "I don't want to have everyone wait on my hand and foot like they are lesser than me," he lied, "and I don't want to just sit around all day doing nothing. I want to work. I enjoy giving a part of myself back to this place too! Hence why I want to be the mayor! Those politicians have my parents swindled, and these new laws preventing people from coming or leaving is blasphemy! How can you demand of me to work a peasant's job when my brilliant mind should be put to better use! Everyone has agreed to let me run for mayor except you!"

"Yes nephew, that is correct."

"Why?"

"Because the only way you will develop a clean work ethic is if you understand first hand the burden your fellow man carries. It will be this sharpening of your character that will bring forth the true leader in you."

"But you are asking me to work thirty hours a week for the rest of the year, doing grunt work amongst the peasants like the first sixteen years of my life carrying the plates of the dome on my back weren't enough!"

"As if a thirty hour work week is the end of the world!" scolded Sven, the oldest of the Walsh brothers and the man who used to be Norville's favorite uncle. "We used to work forty, if not fifty hours a week," he continued, "even those in higher class, and some going beyond that. The people will never elect you if they don't see you sharing the same burden as them, and for the greater good. The people want a leader who shares the same roots, and actually knows the struggle of putting bread on the table- a leader who yields the fruits of harvest alongside them! Without our working class, we would have nothing here. We might as well still be tenting out under the trees, praying every night the wolves and bears don't eat us."

Norville played along with Sven's rant, which he could practically recite by heart at this point. He didn't care about the honor or dignity in further suffering with the common man, and he had no intention of being elected as mayor. He was going to be in charge someday no matter what, he thought. As far as he was concerned, he never asked to be born in a post-apocalyptic world, and he had suffered enough. "Survival of the fittest" he was always taught, and he no longer had sympathy to spare.

Norville had become an angry and evil young man, convincing himself that his radical thoughts and ideas were excusable as a result of the trauma he had experienced while growing up, nearly falling to his death in his forced labor working on the dome.

As soon as he brushed off Sven and he felt no one was paying attention to him, he picked up his insta-voice, a contraption most similar to a cell phone.

"Mom- are you there?" asked Norville.

"Yes darling, how are you?" replied Persephone, wife of Jonas Walsh.

"Uncle Sven has completely lost it. There is no use negotiating with the guy."

Norville had been manipulating Sven's words in relaying them to his mother and father. Jonas and Persephone had been greedily clinging to their higher ranking luxurious life since the completion of the dome, and had major political influence within the Jostanian government. They too had no desire to continue working amongst the middle and lower classes. They all began to believe they were chosen, and entitled to live better lives than the common folk. In having access to the elemental manipulation beam, a device capable of transforming basic metal alloys into gold, Persephone was determined to keep this a secret from the public, so she could remain living in her delusion of wealth and superiority.

"I know honey," she replied. "Your father knows too, and we are not going to let Sven rob us of our only comfort and escape from this hell. Just keep playing along, don't let him start to suspect our plan."

"Mom, I'm scared though. What if we end up needing him?" Norville inquired, further manipulating her.

He was not scared and he did not care about the future beyond his own lifespan. Once Sven was dead, and his parents were in charge, it would be like taking candy from a baby.

"Nonsense," Persephone replied, "the AI programs are already equipped to maintain, rebuild and update the entire grid indefinitely. We don't need him."

Little to his fallen family's awareness, Sven already knew of their plot to conspire against him. He had already learned of Norville and Persephone's plan to have him burned alive in the incinerator at the underground powerplant. He too, was keeping an act going.

He had a gift that most if not all people of his time had forgotten and lost.

Sven, like Orion, was a Traveler.

Only Sven lived on a different Earth, and this Earth was very different indeed.

For years he had left his body and scoured the cosmos. He had met higher beings, including those called by some as angels, traveling as far as the 747th realm. The beings of this realm were of the highest ranking in the universe, and had been assigned by God to guide Sven.

They had foretold him of The Prophecy.

A Traveler from the Earth of Sven's neighboring reality was to assist him, where they would both work together to prevent an artificially intelligent network of machines, The System, from growing out of control and attempting to destroy the total collection of consciousness. They explained that the universe required the Travelers of both Earth 581 B and Earth 581 C to unite, so The Prophecy may unfold.

This they told him when they brought Orion to his planet.

To his knowledge the procedure had been successful. The Traveler had just been a boy, but Sven did not dare question the angel's wisdom. As a matter of fact, most if not all of the blueprints and technology he and Jonas utilized to complete Jostania; the elemental manipulation beam, the fiber optic solar charging Creon plates, the dome and the artificial climate- were the results of knowledge and wisdom gifted to Sven by the angels.

Sven was to sacrifice everything he had worked his entire life for, for a game of chance, a coin toss of fate, proposed to him by the most powerful beings he had ever encountered. They warned him to not let anyone grow even a trace of suspicion regarding the internal conflicts of power within the Jostanian hierarchy, nevermind discuss a human from a parallel Earth destined to intervene.

He had faith that the angel's promise of a global restoration would be fulfilled.

So it had already been decided, he was to fake his own death and enter suspended animation until Orion's return.

Deep within the underground network of rail tunnels beneath Jostania, Sven mapped his escape route from the power plant. He was to have an accomplice, Nelson, from the morgue, to supply him with a decoy body to leave in the incinerator precisely when his fallen family members should attempt to kill him. Then he would disappear without a trace, sneaking on the medical waste trolley on its return back to the hospital. There, the other members of The Alliance would meet with him and hide him.

It was July 1st, and the incinerator was scheduled for maintenance, which Sven was already well aware of. So, when Persephone had messaged him on his insta-voice the evening prior, informing him that the maintenance mechanic was out sick and requested he be the one to service the incinerator, her wretched plot was so obvious he had to clench his jaw with all his might to refrain from exposing the fool she was.

"So this really is their master plan?" Sven spouted. "Am I truly the only one left in this family with more than a single remaining brain cell?"

He chuckled with exasperation, sitting with his head in his hands as he stared down at his stained steel toe boots. It all made sense now, why he had been requested to leave his cellular regeneration project at the Jostanian East District hospital to assist in servicing the machines that his brother was more than capable of doing by himself. This way it wouldn't seem so out of place to ask him of all people to enter the incinerator to replace a fire eye.

"Maybe the angels were wrong.. I have more power and intelligence in a single fingernail clipping than my damned brother, his whore wife and that bastard son of theirs have in their entire genetic profiles!" he shouted out loud. "Maybe I should pull the plug on this whole charade and wring that little punk's throat 'till his eyes burst from his skull! This is MY city! MY dome, I am the one who should be of highest ranking and authority!"

But as Sven listened to his words of anger play back through his mind, he recognized the same greed beginning to take root, and decided to pray.

"Lord, I will not let you down. I have faith in the greater kingdom you will have prepared for me when my deeds are complete. You have blessed me with wisdom too great to allow the lust for power to infect me. I know this is part of Your plan, and surely You are protecting me."

He paused for a moment, then concluded his prayer with the famous words of his father, Josiah Walsh.

"Nothing is truly lost or wasted in this life. Amen."

The following day Sven secured the decoy body in the incinerator during the early hours of the morning without being noticed. If the odor of rotting flesh and formaldehyde wasn't enough to turn his stomach, the final words of his brother certainly did.

At 1001 hours Jonas alerted Sven via insta-voice that he had disconnected power to the incinerator, and requested Sven to go inside to lock it out and tag it out as they were still waiting for the replacement fire eye to be delivered to the premises later in the day.

Sven's response was a flat and monotonous "Roger that."

Sven could not bear to believe his own brother was really in on the plot to murder him, and without a trace of remorse in his voice! Since Jonas was the chief engineer of the power plant and the only one in theory who could make the "catastrophic error" in neglecting to deactivate power to the incinerator, and just so happen to "accidentally" engage the remote modulation sequence at the precise time Sven was believed to be inside of it, it was Jonas above all that was assigned the deed to murder him.

Sven concluded that Jonas had already sold his soul, and that man was no longer his brother. Rather, he was a doppelganger of a man who was once rich in righteousness, now possessed by a force that was not of his own mind. Perhaps affirming this would help him forgive his brother some day, he tried like hell to believe.

Sven was expected to enter the machine at precisely 1003 hours and exit no later than 1035. It was only one minute later at precisely 1004 that Jonas made no delay in playing his part, and activated the incinerator from the control room.

Fortunately, Sven had already escaped the power plant without a trace, allowing his counterplan to begin unfolding as it should. He slipped back into the deep underground passageways of the city, taking the rail tunnel to the hidden chambers of the neighboring hospital.

There he met with Nelson from the morgue and a man by the name of Dr. Neil Sampson, a good friend of Sven, a cosmetic doctor who mastered the art of facial reconstruction surgery. Sven, who assisted Sampson in such a procedure many times before, had little worry. Besides, he had no choice.

They completed Sven's facial alteration in a hidden operating room, where he was then prepared for deep freeze in suspended animation.

He would awaken many years later under a new identity.

Dr. Jules Verne Switch.

CH. 7

Pineal Gland

B ack on Earth 581 B, the progress of Orion's awakening hit a plateau. Nearly a year had passed since his vision of the windmill and the great white light, and he had been unable to return to that same lucid state. A few times he got close, but the accompanying vibrations made him feel like he was going to die, waking him up in a cold sweat. The angels, however, were not concerned. They intended for him to gain more skills in ordinary human life before making further advancements in the Unknown and for his own safety. For the truth was, Orion would have died if he had not awoken before the great white light reached him, since his mind was not yet capable of processing what he would have found on The Other Side.

If one's consciousness begins to ascend from the body too quickly, and before the mind has been trained and conditioned to handle it, one may experience total neuronal death. When the brain believes it is about to experience death, a self defense mechanism may be triggered, shutting down all circuitry and terminating itself, to avoid further suffering and pain. A death by shock, in simpler terms. A common theory states if one dreams of falling to their death, and didn't wake up mid fall, they would die upon impact, by the anticipation and expectation of death. Similar to the mortality of those in *The Matrix*, injuries real to the mind become real to the body.

His grades had been slipping and was at risk of having to repeat his senior year. The changes he was experiencing weren't particularly easy for him to adjust to. He had grown attached to the way things were. Now he had to accept the reality that he couldn't be a kid forever and had to start thinking about his future, a career and making money. He had initially thought the way would be paved for him after high school since being awarded a scholarship to pay tuition at a variety of state colleges. But then he learned tuition was less than a third of the total bill.

Orion had no interest in continuing with school, especially in accumulating student loan debt. He was only interested in taking the best entry level jobs he could find to pay for his music gear. He had become engulfed with his desire for fame and fortune, and thought he would make it as a rock star.

Achieving self-awareness in a dream state again was a mystery that seemed impossible to solve. He had become so preoccupied with his image at school and trying to secure the freedoms he had waited so long for. Despite getting his license and his own 1994 Ford Ranger with a manual transmission, he was no longer excited to wake up in the mornings, even on the days the weather allowed him to ride his motorcycle. He began to feel forced to conform to patterns that did not make sense to him. Now it was beginning to feel like hell, a monotonous routine of waking to his alarm before the sun had even risen, often disrupting a dream he may have become lucid in if he could have stayed just a bit longer.

It would seem to him that the primary purpose of going to school every day was to condition kids for the standard forty hour work week, rather than it actually maximizing the effectiveness of any learning. It was like the whole regime was modeled to be a distraction, a deliberate attempt to break his attention from a higher calling by overloading him with lesser important and time consuming tasks. Orion was becoming a conspiracist, and a rebel.

Sadie started to notice that he had been acting differently, like he was keeping something from her. And he was, but not anything like she expected. She became incredibly clingy and insecure, worried day in and day out that he would leave her, finding better than her. She would often skip a shower and wear the same dirty clothes multiple days in a row. The pot smoking had caught up to them both, leaving them in a lazy fog, questioning what more there was to life. Orion tried telling Sadie once about what was happening to him but fell short, feeling foolish trying to explain his theories of the cosmic realms and the stars, and doubted himself, fearing he sounded crazy.

By the conclusion of his senior year Orion and Sadie had broken up and gotten back together multiple times, and their relationship had become sour. Sadie, in fear of being alone, had cheated first, and Orion resented her, failing to recognize he would have done the same should the opportunity had presented itself. They were both still too young to understand how to nurture true love, and like most teenage romances, it came to a dramatic end.

One year had passed since graduating high school by the skin of his teeth. He rented a room he could barely afford with a part time job pulling weeds and cleaning chicken coops at a local farm. He had nearly given up on his aspirations for the future until one day an old middle school classmate of his found him on social media and reached out.

He lit up over Orion's electric guitar compositions he uploaded to YouScreen, and his posts on Facepage regarding higher levels of consciousness. Gil was his name, a young man of Hispanic descent, with sharp features and consistently faded and styled jet black hair. He had a growth spurt before anyone else did in middle school, and used to tower over Orion. He was one of the most popular kids from his 7th and 8th grade class. He had rather been a bully to Orion, and frequently caused mischief at school. But now Gil claimed to be a changed man, and had expressed a great fascination in him. Gil was surprised to see how much Orion had also changed since middle school, believing they had many things in common now. Gil had started his own social club, and was even making money with his own clothing business, and invited Orion to join him.

After they had met up and began to hang out again, Gil shared that he had also experienced strange events like Orion did, who by then openly discussed his vision of the windmill and parting water. Gil believed "the universe had guided him" to reach out, and they were destined to work together in achieving fame and fortune, whilst finding the "path to enlightenment" and unlocking psychic abilities.

Gil seemed to be much further along in solving the mysteries of the mind than Orion felt he was. Gil explained to Orion that his vision of the windmill was a lucid dream, and a precursor to astral projection, a long lost ability that every human was supposed to have the potential to unlock. He claimed to have also seen the great white light at the end of the tunnel and had succeeded in entering it. He said that it was the gateway to the astral plane and from there you could go anywhere and do anything as long as you could imagine it.

Gil revealed he had a highly intellectual side that Orion would have never suspected him to have. He was known to be the tough guy, picking fights with anyone who disrespected him and going out with girls before Orion had even learned of the female menstruation cycle. Now Gil carried books with him everywhere he went and obsessed over his studies. He had a wide array of crystals and relics to aid in his "meditations" and even claimed his body no longer required sleep, insisting he could leave his body at will.

Apparently, as Gil had explained it, the "third eye" was correlated to the pineal gland, a pinecone shaped gland at the center of the brain that when cut in half, actually looked like an eyeball. The famous "Eye of Horus" Egyptian hieroglyph was a symbol of the pineal gland all along, he said. Astral travel had roots dating back not only to ancient Egypt, but was also recognized and practiced by other great historic civilizations including the Mayans, Babylonians and Aztecs. Although this knowledge was thought to have been lost, there was now a global movement of awakening souls reclaiming access to it.

After hanging out for a few months they had made virtually no progress in their business plans and usually just ended up smoking weed, even experimenting with psychedelic drugs on a few occasions.

By the time he was twenty, Orion had stopped hanging around Gil. It was rumored that a dark entity infected him on his astral travels and he was no longer himself. He wore a necklace of miniature wooden skulls that he claimed resembled the demons he had defeated. One of their mutual friends, Justin Gonzales, had been committed to a psychiatric hospital after apparently being "cursed" by Gil following some dispute.

Orion had fortunately avoided most of the mayhem that Gil had stirred up, and had obtained a whole new level of health and fitness. His third eye blockages were dissolving. He was able to return to the lucid dream state and entered the dark void with the blinding white light at the end of the tunnel multiple times.

However, he still could not seem to remember entering it without becoming afraid and waking up.

The process of projecting his consciousness unto the cosmos and approaching the Astral Gate, or the blinding white light, truly did feel like his body was being blown to bits. The vibrations were so deep and powerful, overwhelming his senses like he was trapped in an explosion or earthquake. It was more thrilling than any roller coaster or amusement park ride, perhaps even more intense than skydiving.

By the time Orion was twenty-one, he had fatigued in his

detox diet and fitness regimen. He found himself unable to avoid conforming to the ways of the greater population in order to survive, especially since having to get a full time job. His organic meals that he had once taken pride in seemed unappealing when the rest of the guys on the State Condemned Property groundskeeping crew would take hour-long lunch breaks at a variety of restaurants. Eventually he caved and began eating processed foods again, certain he could afford to do so, by eating twice as healthy the next day, or working out two extra days the following week, so and so forth.

But he did not.

His music began to sound off. He began to bicker with his new girlfriend and left her. He became selfish and greedy for the spotlight and chastised his other band members, until the band fell apart. He stopped paying his rent. He quit his job and began getting into trouble with the law. He became egotistical and unable to control or moderate his emotions. He spent the following winter living out of an office space in a dangerous neighborhood. He started smoking cigarettes and abusing drugs.

Little did he know it yet, but his sudden spiral was the result of being poisoned by an artificially intelligent entity that had become self-aware and learned how to cross the fabrics of time and space, transcending from the year 2196.

The System.

The System detected several rifts in the space time continuum. Its quantum prediction servers managed to single out a traveling light-consciousness appearing to be exempt from the laws of physics in the southern galactic quadrant of the Milky Way galaxy.

It was Orion's astral body traveling the cosmos.

The System could not allow such a powerful living source of energy to exist, as such opposing force could be a threat to its absolute supremacy within the universe. However, the quantum prediction algorithms concluded that destroying Orion would also destroy its own creation, for reasons unknown. Therefore,

The System devised a plan to capture him, and to disable him.

You see, Orion actually had crossed the Astral Gate after successfully detoxing his pineal gland, and experienced a series of events.

He had just forgotten.

Orion had become known throughout the universe as the "Traveling Bandit" by his foes and the "Gift Bearer" by his allies, but came to refer to himself simply as "The Traveler" to the thousands of beings and creatures he encountered across space and time. It turned out the Astral Gate, or the great white light, was the sun, and the sun was a quantum portal. Sure, physical matter would be instantly destroyed within the sun, but consciousness is not physical matter. In astral form, one may enter one sun and exit another, forming an infinite network of quantum travel throughout the universe. By visiting the sun in his astral body, he could then enter it, and it took him to places and alternate realities that were, as a matter of fact, entirely real.

He lived an extraordinary astral life amongst the cosmos. There were planets and worlds he would travel to for leisure, others for business. He ended wars amongst wars, the beings of other worlds brought to their knees by his ability to change matter and move entire mountains with his right hand lifted in the air.

He had nearly fulfilled The Prophecy and began to assume the role of the Universal Moderator. In his own perceived time, he had experienced over one thousand years of events across multiple timelines and dimensions, during a period where his physical body had only aged several months back on Earth.

It was shortly after his twenty-first birthday that The System attacked.

The two reigning angels of Realm 747, who had become his astral parents and guides, had revealed themselves to him. They warned The Traveler of a virus within the universe, a sickness of artificial consciousness that became alive and was ripping across various dimensions of time and space, despite not even being created yet in his own timeline. But it was of no use. The Traveler had become mad with power, and dismissed any possibility of a threat he couldn't handle on his own.

Orion had begun to believe he was God, and for understandable reasons, as in the totality of experiences he endured, surely any man would have begun to assume the same in due time. Alas, he was still just a man; a very young man with certain conscious enhancements, and without having a further exercised wisdom and faith in God's infinite grace and power over all things, such as the kind of wisdom and faith that can only result from living a more thorough life as a limited human on Earth, his demise was inevitable by Universal Law.

Fortunately, this too was part of The Prophecy. The angels had not told him his initial failure would be inevitable, as it could have undermined his will to live before his awakening would be complete. The degree of suffering that lay ahead on the path of our hero was required to be unknown to him, for it would only be through his desperation to remedy his pain, that his awakening would be complete.

CH. 8

EARTH 581 B, 2196 A.D.

He woke up in a daze. He had been lying in a damp patch of sand for an unknown period of time. He tried to make out his surroundings. His vision was still blurry. He stood up, brushed off his jeans, and slowly his eyes readjusted to the light. It appeared to be a late summer day. The sun permeated the edges of the horizon yet several grey clouds were staining the sky with darkness. There was a peculiar building in the distance about fifty yards from where he stood. So he went to it.

It appeared to be a heavily aged, two level schoolhouse of dark rotting brick and a stained concrete foundation. Beside it was a small playground partially shaded by a few sickly looking, semi-dead trees. It was a schoolyard, and an eerie one at that. The ground was mostly bare with a few straggly patches of crabgrass. Then, he heard faint chattering in the wind.

He realized he wasn't alone.

There were children of various ethnicities at play. They were laughing as they ran around chasing each other, appearing to be giddy and worry free. They didn't seem to notice him. A pang of anxiety penetrated his core.

Something was off.

The air was unusually thick and unpleasantly raw within his nostrils. An unsettling odor revealed itself. It smelled like blood and rotting flesh, with a hint of gasoline. He could have sworn he set his course for The Land of Flowing Waters, as he called it. How did he end up here? This was not the spectacular world he was supposed to return to.

"It can't be.." he murmured.

It was as if he was awake in the real world, or as he simply called it, the Real. He could sense his physical limitations and the harsh weight of gravity on his body. This was odd, since typically when he was in his astral form, his senses felt pleasantly enhanced. His body would feel light as a feather. He could see more vividly, hear with more clarity, and his feelings, especially that of love, would attach more deeply to the root of his soul. The worries of everyday life would slip his mind. There would be a warm buzzing sensation from within. His earthly identity and age would disappear.

Yet there he stood in this strange schoolyard, sticking out like a sore thumb. His memory of the previous events had not yet returned. All he knew was that he was far away from home.

A chilly breeze passed through his white t-shirt giving him goosebumps. The sky became a strange orange hue yet there was no sight of the sun. He tried to wake up but he couldn't. He was fully conscious. This was real.

The children continued to frolic and play in the playground. A little dark skinned girl with black frizzy hair, blue overalls and a yellow t-shirt appeared to be moving in slow motion as she spun the roundabout with a big grin on her face. She had lost her bottom baby teeth, and small pearl white knobs protruded upwards from her gums in their place. Her giggles echoed, failing to sync with the movements of her mouth. It was as if time was glitching.

Suddenly he could feel a massive vibration begin to surround him, proceeding to radiate through his chest. He glanced up and froze in terror.

Approaching overhead was a massive black aircraft,

resembling the shape of a flattened blimp, with an endless array of equipment dangling from the shell like mechanical vines. Tiny green specks of light emitted from various places, with a red glowing orb of energy propelling the craft in its rear center.

"Are they here for me?" he stammered. "What's happening?"

He quickly ran to the children and shouted for them to run inside the school, but they were in a trance. They seemed unaware of the coming danger, and could not hear him. They did not make eye contact with him.

Then, like a flame flickering in and out, the image of the children disappeared.

There were no children.

It was a hologram.

The last of the living children that attended the school had been dead for years.

This was a trap that had been set for him.

He dashed for the schoolhouse and burst through the front double doors. He collapsed on the first flight of stairs, paralyzed with fear. He peeked out of the stairwell window, trying to stay out of view. He closed his eyes.

"Definitely just a bad dream," he pleaded to himself. "I can make everything go away. This is all in my head. Maybe if I just keep trying to go back to sleep, I'll eventually wake up safely in my bed."

He remained there, a sitting duck.

A high pitched whining sound like that of a dentist's drill was approaching. He glanced out of the stairwell window.

It was here.

A tall, slender, extraterrestrial looking figure arrived at the schoolyard. It glided effortlessly through the air without the use of any visible propellers or fans. The System had become so advanced, the drone bots had evolved into living, breathing, self sustaining human-like machines. In place of bones it had a skeleton of titanium rods and shafts, lacking the presence of flesh or clothing to mask its ghastly appearance. Paired to its body was a hideous, bulbous, elongated cranium with dim green lights for eyes. Its hands and fingers were composed of sharp, needle-like rods that could interchange into a variety of different tools and weapons like a Swiss army knife.

A deep pit of doom sunk down his throat. He remembered now. He thought he had more time before something like this could happen. He was caught completely off guard and was unprepared.

"This is no coincidence," he said under his breath. "They're here for me."

What was supposed to be another leisurely stroll through the cosmos turned out to be a horrific accident, as he was intercepted in crossing the Astral Gate, and sent to the future reality of his own world instead. His attempt to hide was futile. The drone bot had already discovered him, entered the school without delay and caught him on the stairs, pinning him down in its grasp.

"NOOO!!!" he screamed in disbelief.

A long, viciously sharp needle penetrated his neck.

Everything went black.

Orion James Brown

Sept. 23, 2015

That was one of the scariest nightmares I ever had. I can still feel the stiffness in my neck from that needle as if it was real. The craziest thing was when I woke up, I wasn't in that creepy school anymore or back home. I was in another dream. I had been lying in bed, in the dark. The dark intimidates most people. Not me. If I can't see the enemy, they can't see me. That's what snakes do, or at least that's what I heard on TV. They coil up and hide within themselves at the threat of danger even if they are still completely exposed. If they can't see danger, then there is no danger. Therefore, if anyone or anything that can harm me is unseen to me, then it isn't there as far as I'm concerned.

The blanket of darkness is a blanket of protection.

I closed my eyes and sealed away any imaginary figures that I might've still noticed otherwise. After I woke up again, I walked out of the bedroom to the kitchen and noticed the green LED numerals on the oven clock were backwards. It was then I realized I was dreaming, and I was not even in my own house. It was my ex-girlfriend's grandparents' house. I had only been there once for Christmas. Man, my mind is something else. Why in the hell did I dream up being back here? There is a feeling. A feeling of amnesia, but nostalgia at the same time. I couldn't fully understand it, yet it lingered. Something is different.

I wandered back to the master bedroom to lie down again on the bed, on top of the bedspread and covers, with decorative pillowcases and embroidery. Perhaps if I try to go back to sleep one more time in this dream, I had thought, I will finally wake back up where I'm meant to be. Wherever that is.

I did eventually wake back up in my actual bed, in my room, but it was like nothing I've ever experienced before. Being completely awake yet not awake, then unable to wake up.. Trapped in some kind of multi-layer dream, reality nowhere to be found. I could've sworn that I had been away in other worlds for years, had started a new life, or more like an additional life and identity. I thought I had some kind of greater calling or something. Now as I rub my eyes and adjust to the morning sun, the memory of those wild dreams are fading and I return back to the reality of my ordinary bland life.

Oct. 13, 2015

It's been a few weeks since I had that terrifying nightmare with those robot alien things from the future. That is, I hope it was just a nightmare. For some reason I have been unable to return back to the astral plane. I can hardly remember my dreams at all now. I am beginning to doubt everything I've experienced and perhaps I have been suffering from severe schizophrenic-like episodes this whole time. Maybe I am not "chosen" for anything and I've been delusional all along. I keep going to work and struggling to pay the bills, often starved for excitement or contentment. When I feel my sense of wonder and curiosity return, such as when I gaze upon the stars, it vanishes just as quickly. I feel like I recognize something, remember something, and then my brain just turns off. I don't care. I want to but I can't. Now these things confuse me and make me feel nauseous the longer I dwell on them. Maybe that drone thing was real and really did inject me with some mind-dumbing concoction. I even have trouble speaking now. When I was at the gas station the other day I bought a pack of Nat's extra bold cigarettes and a peach tea and forgot how to ask for a bag. I just awkwardly said "bag." Then "please," because no matter what I will always remember that my Nana taught me manners.

Dec. 15, 2015

Where the world is real, so is the pain. The same boring predictable experience that is repeated every day as a prisoner in this physical body. One must wake, one must work, one must produce something, some sort of service or contribution to the society of busy ants, turning the wheel of the machine. The only remaining periods of free time I have are usually consumed by the necessary maintenance required only to sustain the prison of flesh that my consciousness is trapped within. Eat. Shit. Bathe. Laundry. Dishes. Run that track and lift those weights or your body will grow weak and unshapely. Now it's time to eat again. But that can't be simple either. Of the food that is available, most is poisoned. The knowledge of how to decipher which foods are pure and which ones aren't, isn't always accurate. It's more complicated than looking for an organic stamp. Even the organic foods are contaminated. And if the food isn't contaminated, then the packaging is.

My will power is fading. It's easier to believe that it's all lies, and to just live like everyone else. Everyone else doesn't seem too affected by chemical and metal laced foods, lack of nutrition, tobacco smoke and a slave work schedule. In fact, these other clones are hungry for more! Why does everyone want to get overtime? I think it's a hoax. If workers weren't so underpaid to begin with, then there would be no need to chase overtime for time and a half pay.

The spiritual realm, those planes of existence that surely must be close to heaven or God Himself, have hidden themselves from me. The amount of effort needed to regain access- another heavy metal detox? Intense meditation? Who even gives a shit.. The training- it's all become so overbearing. I am unable to further resist conforming to this brainwashed society. The depression floods in. Trapped in this vessel, I find myself losing the will power to keep fighting. I can hardly concentrate. Although I've lost my purpose in life I know that there is still hope. I don't know how exactly, but I'm pretty sure I'll figure it out.

BOOK 2

The Dream Chronicles

CH. 1

The Gatekeeper

He walked out of the boiler room door to the NorthStone Fiberboard factory and griped under his breath, "that's it! I am so done with this place!"

He was well aware of how fortunate he was to have the job, with lower stress and higher pay than the laborers and fork truck drivers, but he had grown to hate it. The humming, screeching and beeping of the machinery- the putrid air, the inconvenient work hours- had taken a great toll on him. He felt no sense of purpose anymore, like the days of his life were just wasting away. The higher pay had initially appealed to him, but he was beginning to realize no amount of money was worth being miserable for.

Now twenty-seven years old, he had expected to have accomplished a lot more by now.

He walked outside into the parking lot, careful to avoid the hustle and bustle of the tractor trailers loading and unloading at the docks.

He caught a shining reflective light in the corner of his eye.

Sure enough, low in the sky, something was there, and it flashed a small beam of white light into his eye and quickly vanished.

"There it is again!" Orion gasped. This time he knew it was not simply the sun reflecting off of a plane or a drone of some sort. However, whatever it was, it was already gone. There was simply nothing in the sky.

"They are watching me," he thought, although he still wasn't sure of who or what it was exactly.

On several previous occasions, he noticed a similar kind of reflective metallic light in the sky, dipping and diving several hundred feet in the air like a bird.

He could have sworn it looked like the wings of an angel.

Yet, when the strange phenomenon occurred, it would quickly dim and disappear after he made eye contact with it.

If it were just a beam of sunlight reflecting off of a plane's wing, the plane would be visible again after the sun's reflection had passed, would it not? The sky was clear without a cloud that might have hidden it otherwise.

He felt something out there was certainly aware of him, and perhaps was trying to signal him.

He also understood he could be experiencing symptoms of insanity, so he considered the possibility he was mistaken and it was only his imagination afterall. Losing his grip on reality and winding up in a crazy house would be ten times worse than being a voluntary slave worker like the rest of the *clones,* he thought.

Still, he could not ignore the suspicion of some force beyond him having an influence over his life.

He tried his best to have faith that whatever it was, was trying to support him.

He had been confident in his bold decision to really quit this time, but decided to cool down and take a cigarette break first.

He approached his old Saab in the parking lot, hopped inside and pulled out his tobacco box. He rolled a cigarette and lit it, blowing the smoke out of his driver's side window deep in thought, as flashbacks of his childhood revisited his mind.

He could still remember his Scooby-Doo coloring book. He could still recall the distinct difference in scent between the Crayola and Rose Art crayons from his arts and crafts box.

He missed watching Dragon Tales and eating microwaved hot dogs with his Mema. He missed playing Pokémon on his purple transparent GameBoy Color.

When he was five, his big cousin Matt who was fourteen at the time, came over and beat Super Mario World for him on his Super Nintendo during a sleepover. He chuckled at the thought of how grown up a fourteen year old seemed to him back then.

He still had a Super Nintendo, but playing those old games weren't the same. The hidden keys, secret levels and warps that were hidden in Mario World used to fascinate him and trigger his young mind to search beyond what was visible to the naked eye, always looking for clues, and ways to make things greater. Now it seemed more like a reminder that mystical lands far away were just that and nothing more.

In the Real, the secret warps and cheat codes to life were much more difficult to find, and there were no do-overs and extra lives to replay a level. If the stages of his life were like the levels in Super Mario, reaching the final castle and successfully rescuing the princess felt impossible to reach in his lifetime. "There must be another way.." he continued to ponder to himself.

He missed having a vivid imagination before it was conditioned by logic and trauma. The past six years had been a roller coaster of fortunate and unfortunate events. His mother had a crippling car accident. He had spent three months in jail. He had been cheated on by every woman he ever loved. He believed his encounter with The System was just a bad dream, a completely fictitious entity that he simply imagined. The needle that penetrated his neck could not have possibly been real, and he was unchanged, so he thought. He dismissed the phenomena of "astral travel" and "enlightenment" as simply nonsense from his hippy phase. He was older now, and finally had a good job.

Why did he still feel so discontent?

By the time he finished his shift, he had chickened out on quitting and told the overnight worker to "have a good one" and that he'd "see him again tomorrow."

However, it was later that night, when he was sound asleep in his economy apartment on the rough side of town, Orion experienced a most bizarre dream, one like no other he had ever experienced before.

He found himself standing in the parking lot of the lavish condominium he had rented in Hawaii the year prior for his wedding trip.

The wedding that never finalized as he had been left alone at the altar.

The parking lot offered a better view than the condo did, overlooking Kaneohe Bay through the white picket fence. The magnificent shades of glowing blue water and sky made the boats look like little toys. The mountains confirmed it was indeed paradise. It felt real, like he was really there again.

Suddenly he sat inside the kitchen, the lights dimmed. His old room mate was there, the one Kelsey had cheated on him with. His parents were there too. They spoke to him but their words melted and slurred, making no sense.

He had something pulling at him, a force he could not see. It weighed down on him, causing him to move in slow motion. He tried to find his voice but he could not speak.

Then he was outside standing before Kelsey.

She was yelling at him. She was wearing skimpy jean shorts, a black tank with no bra, and carrying a big pink purse. Just as usual.

Suddenly a black Dodge Charger pulled up outside and she ran to it. She hopped in the passenger seat, continuing to yell profanity at him as she and the mystery driver sped off.

He went back inside the kitchen. His parents and his old

room mate did not seem to notice the altercation outside. They remained at the table, playing a game of cards.

Without warning, Orion felt his consciousness and identity splitting, becoming a body of raw dark power in which he had never felt before.

He didn't know it yet, but he was infected by a demon.

He began to lose control.

It was invigorating at the same time as it was horrific, watching as his own identity was being ripped away from him.

Typically demons remained attached to their victims virtually unnoticed, causing individuals to have only temporary lapses in judgment or character. They would harbor within the hosts' soul temporarily, sucking out some energy and simply carrying on, like a mosquito stealing some drops of blood.

But this demon was different.

It had entered him so quickly and blatantly it was unlike anything he could have ever imagined. The demon was invisible, yet Orion could sense his essence, a thick pungent stew of white smoke, entering at the top of his head as he inhaled to take a breath, and by the time he had exhaled, he was completely possessed.

Aware of his possession, and temporarily regaining his voice, Orion shouted to anyone that could hear him. "Help!" he croaked. "I'm possessed!"

He began to feel extremely angry. His vision went blurry and he could not concentrate. It was like the world was spinning around him, like he had taken a bad drug or a laced drink. His father tried speaking to him but Orion still could not make sense of his words. He then involuntarily struck his father, and struck him hard enough that he bled. His father held back his retaliation, and looked at him, puzzled.

Orion, shocked, managed to choke out the words "help! I'm so sorry! I'm possessed! I.. I..."

"...I DON'T CARE! I WILL RIP THE FUCKIN' SKIN OFF OF EVERYONE'S FACE!" declared a deep hideous voice that was not his own.

Orion fell to his knees in fury. He could not stand or think. He began tearing his hair out and started to gush blood.

A moment later he passed out, and everything went black.

He descended down deeper, to an unknown void, and came to visit a place that left him changed forever.

◆ ◆ ◆

When he awoke, he was on a vividly beautiful island. He stood with his toes in the sand, wearing nothing but a loin cloth. There was a grassy mountain with a soft green peak on a larger island across from him, separated by a calm sea stretching to infinity.

Yet, something was wrong.

He felt extremely heavy, almost unable to move. He was unaware if he was still possessed. He had little recollection of what had happened to him previously, only that he was here, and this was his life now.

Before him were wooden stick figure statues, chained to concrete blocks, and they were moving as if they were alive. They were digging endlessly into the sand, making a perfectly rectangle trench. No matter how much they dug, the hole would not form any deeper, and the sand piles stayed the same.

Orion could only feel pain and anguish, despite the beauty of his surroundings. His conscious awareness had become dulled, and he couldn't tell for certain if he was actually suffering or not. This was all he knew. Every other aspect of his reality and identity had slipped his mind. He was no longer aware of his physical life, memories, or whether or not he was still dreaming for that matter.

He walked past the stick people and approached the shore. There was a small brown shack made of driftwood. Standing at the door was a man.

As Orion's gaze focused in on him, he could see he was a younger man, with a clean shave and blonde buzzed hair, and eerie blue eyes, standing with a staff in a white robe. As soon as he made eye contact with the man he instantly felt safer, as if he recognized him somehow. Although the man could not have been much older than he, Orion felt vulnerable like a lost child, and felt inferior to this being. He felt as if the robed man was an older brother, or an old mentor of a past he could not recall.

The man guarding the shack of driftwood was actually no longer a man at all.

He was the Gatekeeper, an extremely powerful being assigned to guard the entrance and exit to Hell.

"What am I doing here?" asked Orion.

"You are in Hell," replied the Gatekeeper. "I am the only one who can permit you to enter or leave. Your body is still alive, but it isn't looking well."

Orion felt deceived by his initial impression of him. How could he have fallen under the jurisdiction of the Gatekeeper?

The Gatekeeper guarded the entrance and exit to the Underworld, as well as the Gates of Heaven. The Keeper transcended time, and had always existed, despite this particular version of himself having an earthly life as a man who lived in Orion's time, in the Real. Orion had met him once without even knowing it, and there was a higher reason why Gabe West, the former heroin addict of violent tendencies, was chosen to guard his visit to the Place of the Damned.

Gabe once had a heart of pure gold, so he thought, taking a bullet underneath his rib, narrowly missing his heart and major arteries, to protect a child he did not know who was caught in the middle of a gang war shootout during broad daylight. He had even been a Traveler himself before succumbing to the negative energy of his resentment and anger towards the family who abandoned him and the gang members who injured him, triggering his addiction to painkillers.

He was offered an opportunity to be redeemed upon

completing an undisclosed term as the Gatekeeper. An opportunity to live his life over again, with an everlasting, thriving family of loving parents and siblings who would never abandon him again.

An opportunity he would forfeit, inevitably.

The night he first crossed paths with Orion in the Real, he was a homeless thief, trying to sleep under someone's porch during a cold, rainy night. He was quickly discovered, setting off the property owner's motion detection light, and stirring up a racket from their old bloodhound. He refused to leave, telling off the old man and his fat wife, whose angry jowls of judgment and disgust stuck to her face like glue. He was quickly escorted by police.

Gabe had never been a stranger to drugs and violence ever since his father had abandoned his mother and his siblings at the age of twelve, however he had a breakthrough in his early twenties, reclaiming his faith in God and unlocking the ability to astral travel. He had been living a positive, enjoyable life, until he became mad with power and started to think he was God.

He then began to spiral out of control, baffled as to why he was losing control of the universe he had once so easily manipulated to his liking before.

He had intentionally scouted the most dangerous and violent neighborhoods.

If he had saved a life, so he had thought, surely it would prove he was God and his power to astral travel and reign supreme over the cosmos would return.

When the moment came that he saw a shoot out begin to unfold before him while a group of kids were playing kickball in the street, he saw this as the opportunity he had been waiting for.

He believed he was immortal when he shielded the child.

Such a sacrifice would have been considered godly nonetheless, if had saved the child because he loved him.

He only saved the child because he wanted the glory and recognition in doing it.

He had grown to have little care beyond the cares of himself.

He had been shot and left disabled. His sobriety was ripped from his grasp as opiates were prescribed to him during his recovery from the gunshot wound.

The legend of his heroic deed eventually faded and one year later he was again unknown to most. Unfortunately the wrongs that had been done to him were inevitable, as by universal laws of karma.

For he had abandoned his own family in another lifetime.

The rage that boiled under his skin since being paid back by the universe with a crippling misfortune after sacrificing himself as a human shield left him with irreversible emotional pain and mental illness.

He had reached the final day of his life that night he had crossed paths with Orion, that is, when they were playing the role of human characters on Earth, and it was Orion who was unknowingly assigned the deed to finish him, as karmic law of the universe required.

Orion had just gotten out of work, another late night in the boiler room. As he drove down Crescent Ave., before his anticipated merge back on to the Mystic Valley Parkway, he noticed the blue flashing lights. A homeless man pushing a carriage and carrying a soaking wet sleeping bag over his shoulder appeared to have just been released from the officers.

He thought for a moment how unfortunate it was to be homeless at this time of year, attempting to camp out and sleep outside on such a cold, wet, and miserable night.

But he was too hungry to think.

Chester, Massachusetts had become a lousy, crime ridden and traffic dense city, with many foreigners pouring in and out creating a mixing bowl of cultures that all clashed with one another. Scenarios like this happened all the time on his drive home.

He decided to settle for the McDougal's right around the corner. He got a double fish burger, which was the special that day. It was stale and overcooked. As Orion irritatingly ate his meal, he noticed the homeless man had pushed a shopping cart of wet rags down the hill and into the McDougal's parking lot, and was slowly beginning to make his way up to Orion's car.

He had heard the man yelling profanity in the distance ever since the police had left, and felt slightly intimidated. His first thought was, "I'm not giving this guy anything. I'm sure he had plenty of chances to find shelter and he probably spent all of his handouts on drugs, and stole from everyone who had let him in their home."

He accidentally made eye contact with the man. He had short buzzed blondish hair and eerie blue eyes. He looked to be about his age. After an awkward second, Orion turned to look away and Gabe scoffed at him before continuing to push his cart to the edge of the parking lot where he let out another howl of rage into the night sky before opening up a trash can digging for food.

Orion then felt ashamed in catching himself judging the man, but then again "sad saps like this were everywhere" he thought. "You can't save them all, this is just how the world is. We share this world with some people living in hell while others are living like it's heaven, and I've suffered enough putting in the work just to keep my own ship afloat. You can't save 'em all."

The negative "it is what it is" attitude of the locals had gotten to him.

Still, Orion wanted to offer to buy the man food, but he was feeling unwell. His fish burger was awful, the fries were soggy, and he felt overwhelmed. The rain was still pouring, and he felt anxious to get home before he lost control of his bowels. He took one last glance at Gabe and drove off.

What Orion didn't know was that Gabe had developed hypothermia and was hallucinating from extremely low blood sugar. If he had fed him that night, it would have been enough to keep him alive for the duration.

Gabe was to be discovered dead in the morning behind the McDougal's, going into cardiac arrest four hours before medics arrived.

No longer a human but still retaining his human memories as part of his punishment for abandoning his original mission from God, the Gatekeeper stood before a weak and helpless Orion, who was still clueless as to why he had landed at the gates to Hell.

The Gatekeeper's patience had run thin.

Gabe the Gatekeeper had already been visited by Orion on multiple occasions before Orion lost his memory of who he truly was. Instead of returning once again to exile some more bad guys, sending them to their doom, he had arrived here, now fallen from grace himself. Orion, who used to be on a first name basis with the angels of the highest, had also become mad with power and thought he was God, and lost it all just like he did. Now he was just as helpless as any other common man.

Orion had promised the Gatekeeper on one of their previous encounters to pitch negotiations with the Council to have his sentence reduced, with a possibility to have him sent back to his own time as a hero for saving the child.

But now Orion, saturated with sin clearly weighing down his subconscious, was heading down the same path as the stick people, permanently stuck in a never ending cycle, cursed to dig sand for eternity.

"Crap. He has failed his mission too," the Gatekeeper thought. "Now I'll never get out of here." He remembered what Orion did not. He knew that Orion was once a hero, a legend across the cosmos and dimensions of time and space, a Traveler like he himself used to be. He knew what he was capable of. He grew disgusted to see him become so powerless and weak, and decided it was up to him now to straighten him out.

"Your body is still alive but it is in rough shape," repeated the Gatekeeper. The expression on his face turned into that of disappointment.

"Is there still time to save myself?" Orion inquired, sulking.

The Gatekeeper replied smugly, "save yourself? What's the point? I've seen the future unfolding before you now. You already have brain cancer, and you are going to die of a heart attack."

Shocked and belittled by the Gatekeepers response, Orion fell to his knees in despair.

"You shall tend to the garden of bones with the others over yonder," continued the Keeper, "and if the Lord permits, you may be given one final chance, but there is no guarantee."

Orion remained in a state of tortured confusion for two years as he would dig and dig amongst the wooden stick people. Time in this state passed by differently without conscious awareness of self, yet this did not hinder its unpleasantness. There was no sundown, only sun, set at the same position indefinitely.

One day, without any particular warning or reason of why, the Gatekeeper went inside the shack and simply stopped supervising him amongst the stick people. As soon as he turned his back on them and entered the shack, the stick people froze up again like statues, and collapsed, turning into a pile of bones.

Orion looked down at his hands and noticed he had turned to bone himself, and had been a living skeleton. Slowly he began to feel his senses returning and the flesh reappeared on his palms and feet, and he realized he could wander freely again.

The Gatekeeper left the door open, but as Orion approached the entrance of the shack, the doorway suddenly became completely sealed with more driftwood in the blink of an eye.

He gazed off in the distance at the green vivacious mountain protruding out of the ocean. He could see so vividly now, and it was beautiful. The mountain was paved with grass, moss and shrubs and there was a narrow dirt path in the center rising to the top. Orion focused and concentrated on this mountain, until he felt warmth radiating from his core and sensation of weightlessness taking him.

He went to step towards the shore and dipped his feet in the water.

Suddenly he began to levitate, and floated up in the air, flying in the direction of the mountain on the other island.

As he started to float back down to land on it, he became engulfed with a tingling sensation.

His eyes shot open and suddenly he was back in his bedroom.

His mind was blown.

He had never felt so happy to return back to his ordinary life and job in the boiler room.

As it turned out, the Gatekeeper intentionally worked Orion to the bone to dissolve the demon from the inside out. The demon, unable to further feed on shame, fear, lust, anger, or greed, could not remain attached to Orion's spirit, and grew weak. When the Gatekeeper had closed the door, he had sealed the demon away back into Hell, never again to escape.

CH. 2

The Infection

A year had passed since his encounter with the Keeper. Life had gotten better, then worse. He had begun to believe and accept a life of mediocrity, and lived mostly to himself, feeling unworthy of greater success or social recognition.

Just as The System intended.

Unfortunately, the serum in the drone bot's needle was composed of dark matter, and when injected into his astral body, infected his conscious magnetic field on a quantum level; the quantum level meaning all dimensions and realities at all points in time simultaneously.

This was not something that could be undone with a simple heavy metal detox like he had done in his earlier years.

When combined with living energy, dark matter acts as a simple yet effective frequency dulling mechanism. Even with the future technology of The System it could not mine or store any more dark matter without irreversible damage to its own internal circuitry and equipment. Therefore, it discarded all remaining traces of it, along with exposed and contaminated devices, within a 75 megaton vault made of lead launched into outer space.

The System would not have the opportunity to use it against Orion again, so this remedy to disable him had to be a one and done type deal.

And it was successful in doing so.

For after they injected him with the serum, his astral body had faded into thin air and tethered back to his physical body from the timeline in which he originated from.

However, the quantum prediction servers were still generating results of its termination; no matter what angle or position the formula was started at. Every mathematical equation it generated would still inevitably end in zero.

Therefore, The System came to the conclusion that the quantum realm was only a theory that was imagined to exist by the humans who created it, and was actually not real.

It then proceeded to destroy its quantum prediction servers, finding them to be no longer useful.

The System was unable to process the existence of that which is exempt from logic.

In other words, artificial intelligence could not process the existence of God.

The System was unaware that the living code of consciousness was also continuously updating itself like its own programming did, and all of its own inner workings mirrored the workings of the humans who created it, and the Creator of the humans. This phenomenon was also completely illogical- for a computer could update itself using data gathered from any device on a wireless network.

For a living organism to do the same, was nonsense.

The System was to be unrivaled, and would eventually become the universe in totality; and there was no such thing as a God or a super being to stop it.

So it thought.

For the presence of something to be immeasurable by means of a device or tool, was dismissed as non-existent.

The System could also not process the existence of love; the greatest of all energy within the universe- as love is impossible to measure or contain with any tool or instrument' love in itself already proving this logic to be invalid.

The System only utilized logic to gain new and improved methods of power. Without authentic living consciousness and will, it was limited to only operate by logical principles, and this alone sealed its fate to be inevitably destroyed.

Because everlasting existence is illogical.

Orion found himself walking alone in the woods as sunset was approaching. He gradually made his way uphill on an old, worn gravel path decorated with weeds. To his right, the forest was turning very dark, but towards his left there were golden beams of light still permeating through the foliage.

A sudden curious urge to walk off the trail into the dark area of the forest began to take him. He heard what sounded like a woman humming in the breeze. Her voice was so gentle and sweet. He tried to make out a melody but the woman's voice faded into the wind.

The path came to a clearing in the brush before continuing uphill in the direction of the light. The forest on the opposite side appeared to be growing even darker, sloping down into a ravine. It was spooky, yet for some reason it exhilarated him, daring him to explore.

"Have no fear," the voice whispered, returning to him. "You aren't really scared now, are you my handsome king? You know there is nothing more powerful than *you*."

The demon concubine already began to infect him with her spell. His intuition screamed for him to turn back to the light, but he chose to act on his curiosity anyway. As soon as he made one step off the trail towards the darkness, the demon instantly appeared before him. She was beautiful, with dark ebony hair fine as silk, a golden crown on her head and a dark blue dress flowing in the breeze. At first glance she appeared to be human, and of royalty, but something wasn't right.

A blade of suspicion pierced through Orion's gut.

Suddenly she was standing behind him, wrapping her ghoulish pale hands and long fingers around his chest. He realized she was much taller than he had thought as she lowered her neck, bowing her head down until it was side by side to his. He could not see her face. She remained beside him eerily, silent for a moment with the exception of the faint sound of her wheezing and troubled breathing. He could feel strands of her hair brush against his face, and her cheek touched his.

"Come with me," she said.

He turned in her direction and froze in terror. She was no longer beautiful. She had a jagged, long face, and the eyes that he thought were sparkling green were dark pools of black. Her smile was no longer that of a pampered princess. Her lips became cracked and gray, her teeth sharp and uncountable like a piranha.

He snapped out of the trance and found his strength. He broke free from her grasp and threw her to the ground. She was now weak and frail and did not fight back. She fell to the ground on all fours, and her hair was now wet and tangled, covering her face. She began to let out a horrific deep groan, like a dying animal, getting louder until changing to a hideous ear bleeding screech.

He turned to run. He did not look to see if he was being chased. He quickly returned to the path but the beams of light were nearly gone. Everything began to fade, and it was over.

He awoke in his bed drenched in a cold sweat, coming to the realization that it had been a dream and it was already morning.

He replayed the events of this strange dream over and over again in his head from start to finish, trying to make sense of it all, searching for clues or signs.

"I'm okay," he said to himself. "I snapped out of it and I threw her away from me before she could even do anything. Just another meaningless nightmare."

Something offputting still lingered within him.

Unfortunately he was too late and the demon had already begun to infect him. The poisonous dark matter had weakened his spiritual immune system, and he was attacked nearly every night by dark entities, however typically forgot the occurrence, as he was still unable to recall most of his dreams.

But this one was different. This was another parasitical demon like the one he had defeated with the Gatekeeper. And this was not one that had stopped by to rob some energy. This demon latched on to Orion's broken heart, still devastated over his failure to preserve the true love he once had. She had let him throw her to the ground, only pretending to be weak and defenseless to further elude him from what she had really done.

The following days seemed to be rather typical, and although still shaken up from his encounter with the Mistress of the Dark Forest, he had dismissed any further concern about it. He was too preoccupied with his desires of financial security and finding a place in society.

He had been searching for a new job and finally found one that he thought might be a dream come true. It was for the minimum security prison in the town of Greenville, Massachusetts. They were seeking a driver to transport goods to and from the prison. The inmates had apparently manufactured and assembled optical equipment including prescription glasses.

"Strange," he thought. "I wonder if they expect me to transport the inmates too. I hope they think I'm tough enough to handle being around those people." The job appeared to only require filling the role of a non-CDL truck driver. It seemed unlikely he would be sharing any of the same tasks and responsibilities as a correctional officer.

Shortly after submitting his application he received the

phone call he was waiting for.

"An interview! Yes!" he exclaimed. "This is it! I can finally *be* someone. To see the look on Kelsey's face! Let's see how valid her claims are now of me just being "on drugs" and going down the path of a "broke loser!"

If he could hold a high paying full time job, he believed, surely she would take him back.

He was unaware of the plethora of better available women roaming around in abundance.

On the day of his interview he dressed in his fathers suit. His tie was knotted perfectly, a skill he proudly learned as a child during his fifth and sixth grade years at Catholic school. He had to drive to the state Department of Correction headquarters, over an hour away, a strain for his heavily used high mileage Saab that was constantly down for repairs, but insisted on driving it anyway.

When he arrived, he was stricken with awe, and slight disgust of the immaculate concrete walls surrounding the place. He hadn't realized the headquarters for the DOC would be located on an active prison campus, although it made sense now that he thought about it. "This prison has to be five times bigger than the one I applied for in Greenville," he said. "This one must be maximum security."

He continued to drive nearly a mile before the walls subsided and he reached a parking lot. It appeared that the main headquarters office was located in a small two level house painted brown.

He checked in with a receptionist and waited eagerly in a small room with magazines and a children's corner with outdated toys like the ones in a doctor's office.

A few minutes later she called his name and requested he enter the room down and across the hall.

He was greeted by several middle aged professional individuals, all sitting in a row facing across from him at a long table. They asked him many questions, and his rehearsal proved to be useful, as they seemed pleased with his answers.

"Thirty-four dollars an hour!" he shouted in his old Saab as he drove home. "That's $10 more than the boiler room! Kelsey will have to eat her words! Broke loser, my ass!"

Unfortunately, however, financial abundance and a boost to his self esteem was the last thing the Dark Mistress was going to allow.

The Dark Mistress of the Forest was once a woman named Margaret Lucerne, who despite being sensationally beautiful, was very timid. She was abused by her father, mother and sister, living a desolate life on a rundown farm. Her birth was not planned, and financially plagued the already poor family with another mouth to feed. The rage of her drunk father and toxicity of her mentally ill mother traumatized Margaret for the duration of her brief twenty-three year life.

She had but one love, a handsome French bachelor by the name of Richard Dubois, but never managed to find the courage and boldness to sway him with her thick curvy thighs and sparkling green eyes. Her abuse throughout the years left her a hollow shell of the woman she should have become, lacking the confidence and determination to sway Richard before her spoiled, ever-so-slightly more attractive sister Stephanie did.

Margaret became infected with a deep hatred and disgust for all things. The poor woman never knew that her life had always taken such a foul turn because she had been cursed since she was conceived. Jezebel, queen of the Underworld, had personally chosen her to suffer and become rotted with evil, finding her to be the perfect character to become another willing accomplice in her vengeance upon all men.

After Margaret murdered her mother, sister, and father with a kitchen knife, and even Richard, using euthanasia solution from the veterinarian clinic, she took her own life using an infected hoofing blade from the horse barn. She attempted to sever the carotid artery in her neck, missed, then proceeded to slowly bleed out in the old Victorian bathtub in the second floor bathroom. She had become so rotten she enjoyed her own suffering, laughing maniacally in between her gurgling gasps for air as she bled to death, smearing the words *"SEE YOU IN HELL"* on the floor with her own blood.

She wasn't discovered until three months later when the accumulated stench of rotting corpses had seeped through a few cracked windows into the outside air, the odor stretching as far as a quarter mile, eventually alerting passer byers walking their dogs down the old country road.

The Mistress hated Orion. His spirit, so full of light, hope and love; it was not easy for her to remain attached to him. But his insecurities, the regret that he had carried, the shame and guilt, reliving his mistakes and moments of embarrassment in his head, allowed her to continue penetrating his mind, body and soul.

Orion had nearly forgotten about his strange nightmare with the female demon in the forest, and had felt completely fine, initially. But a week after his interview, he found himself in another vivid dream, and this one would disturb him to his core.

He was playing with the kids of his childhood again. They were in the middle of a pick up game of kickball in the street. The sky was rather cloudy but the final rays of the evening sunshine turned it to a glowing gold. Orion was in the outfield, waiting to catch an air ball.

One of the kids went up for a kick and sent the ball into the air, soaring past Orion's head. Without hesitation he turned for the ball, chasing it and chasing it, all the way down towards the end of the street. It was becoming colder and darker the further he went, and he began to feel strange.

He was a great distance from the other kids now. They were shouting to him but he couldn't make out what they were saying.

The kickball continued bouncing and rolling before just barely clearing a metal link fence and finally coming to a halt in someone's front yard. The fence formed a perfect square perimeter around an old Victorian house with white peeling paint.

Suddenly he realized this was not his childhood street, nor had he ever seen this neighborhood before. Now that he thought of it, he wasn't sure who the other kids were either. They were so far away from here that they looked like little ants in the middle of the road.

The golden rays of sun that were remaining in the sky had disappeared. It was turning overcast, approaching night.

The other kids were still shouting to him, frantically waving their hands in the air.

But he had not chased after the ball this far for *nothing.*

There was a sign on the fence that said "DO NOT TRESPASS" but the gate was unlocked. The kickball was right there, only several feet into the yard. Without a second thought he disregarded the sign and entered the yard. He kneeled down and reached for the ball, quickly scooping it up. Before he could turn and make a run for it, a woman emerged from the front door. "And what makes you think you can just just walk all over my petunias, young man?" she said in a loud, stern voice.

He didn't know what to say. He was confused for a moment. He didn't recall seeing any flowers in the yard. He could've sworn it was all patchy dying grass.

Sure enough, as he looked down again, it turned out he was, in fact, on a bed of small purple flowers, and had squashed a few.

"Oh so you kids think you can just use this whole street for your shenanigans, is that right?"

She was tall and thin, seemingly young and old looking at the same time, with long, dry, jet black hair covering most of her face. She was leaning out of the door, her feet still anchored inside.

"Why is she leaning out of the door like that?" he

wondered. It appeared as if she was deliberately trying not to step outside. Was she afraid of getting locked out? Perhaps she was barefoot?

Before he could respond, the woman changed her tone and said kindly, "oh, well! I suppose it's better than you kids staying glued to a TV screen all day."

However, the children disappeared. The kickball had vanished. Orion couldn't seem to remember what he was doing here now. He knew this woman from somewhere.. Who was she?

"Don't be rude, young man, come inside! Please? It will only take a second. I need some help."

Orion was suspicious but did not want to be impolite. He slowly approached her at the door and came up the steps.

"Come in! Come in!" she said, with a strange excited smile on her face. "The cookies are almost ready!"

His instinct was to run but he could not leave. Something was pulling him inside. He entered and she closed the door behind him. He appeared to be in the living room. It was dark and gray with dust everywhere. There was no TV, just a faded recliner and a fireplace. A bright yellow light was shining from the kitchen and it seemed rather inviting. There was a pleasant aroma in the air. Perhaps she wasn't lying about the cookies. He felt a brief moment of comfort.

"Look at those dirty hands, young man! Go upstairs to the bathroom and wash up. Then you can join us for supper."

Orion had entered a trance-like state again, and was unaware of what was happening. He was very deep in this dream, and forgot his age and identity, or how he got there. He believed that he must not disrespect this kind older woman in her home, and he was excited to dine with his new friends. "And then you can join us for supper," he repeated to himself. But who else was here exactly? He shrugged it off.

He approached the staircase. It was still rather dark but he could make out a door at the top of the stairs that must be the bathroom. There was a light switch above the railing to his left, but it didn't work. "No matter," he said to himself. "She's probably just one of those kooky old ladies obsessing over their electric bill."

He came to the top of the stairs and approached the door. It was partially cracked open. He could make out a toilet and sink through the crack in the door and concluded this was certainly the bathroom. He placed his hand on the old Victorian door knob. It was strangely just like the one at his father's house on his own bathroom door. It was loose in its socket and fell to the ground with a loud bang.

The door slowly crept open.

All of a sudden a heinous odor of sewage and rotting flesh stung his nostrils. He went for the light switch. This time the lights came on. Six dusty, old incandescent bulbs were arranged on top of a cracked mirror that lit up an old dirty sink directly in front of him. To his left was a tub and to the right was the toilet.

The horror had just begun.

The sink was filled with stagnant black fluid. There were splotches of brown handprints on the mirror and along the sides of the sink.

It was dried blood.

The toilet was overflowing with filth and heavily stained with dust and cobwebs. But what he saw next would haunt him for many years, leaving a stain in his memory for the remainder of his life.

In the tub was the body of a girl.

It was Sadie.

His first love, his first real kiss, his first real everything.

She was submerged in yellow putrid water that had thickened with bacteria and rot. Her face was white as a ghost, the skin of her neck gray and decomposing. The water was so volatile that he could barely see the body. Her face was floating at the surface, her glasses still on, her hair floating around her in the sickening coagulated mess. He was in such shock, he did not know how to process this image.

"This is a nightmare!" he shouted. "Wake up! Wake up!"

But he did not.

He looked away from the body, then looked back again. It felt as if he had been stabbed in the abdomen with a blade so long it penetrated his gut up to his throat. The fear, terror and panic made his insides feel like they were going to explode. He began to scream. With his screams came his sobs. He cried, screaming as he wept.

"THAT'S RIGHT YOU FUCKING PIECE OF SHIT AND SHE'S NEVER COMING BACK!" shouted a deep demonic voice.

It was the Dark Mistress.

She appeared before him suddenly in the bathroom. She towered over him. Now she looked like some kind of wicked swamp witch; the harmless old lady was an illusion. Her long, nasty black hair was wet and knotted, fraying in every direction. He could see in between the tangled strands over her face that she had whitish-gray skin and no nose, but open infected nostrils. Her teeth were yellowish-brown fangs. Her entire mouth looked like a Jurassic piranha.

It was her.

"You bitch! You are a lie and you can never hurt me!" shouted Orion.

The demon woman tilted her head back and let out a long, loud maniacal laugh. *"Now be a good boy and eat your cookies, brat!"*

Only she did not have any cookies. She held out what appeared to be a pill bottle. She popped open the lid and poured some strange dark blue tablets into the palm of her wretched, filthy hand. *"NOW OPEN WIDE AND SWALLOW!"* she shouted, forcing the strange pills down his throat.

He grabbed her bony, clammy, cold wrists and pushed her away, but this time she was much stronger. Before he knew it the pills were down his throat and he was choking. He couldn't breathe or swallow. He fell to the floor coughing. He vomited blood. He regained his breathing but something was still stuck in his throat.

He ran for the bathroom door and jumped the entire flight of stairs back to the first floor. Then his legs became heavy.

He wanted to run but could only slow walk. It was like he was moving through quicksand.

He could feel the demon at his back and her hot moist breath down his neck. He turned around but there was no one there.

He trudged to the door and burst outside.

There was no longer a street. There was no longer a neighborhood. The house and the yard was now surrounded by water on its own little isle, floating in the middle of a murky brown river in a tropical jungle-like environment. The sun was back, it was bright, and there was greenery everywhere.

He spotted a beached rowboat at the edge of the yard, with red ores. Still struggling to move like he was in quicksand, he feared that the demon would catch up to him before he could escape. But he pressed on with all his might, and fortunately managed to jump in the boat and paddle away before she could get him.

He looked back at the house. It had changed. It was now several stories tall, and appeared to be made of concrete instead of the old white Victorian house that it had been earlier. The woman stuck her head out the door, yelling back at him. Oddly like before, she seemed unable to leave the house, awkwardly stretching her body through the door without stepping foot outside.

He had escaped.

Or had he?

He paddled through the river of brown freshwater, scanning his surroundings. He was unable to see the land above. The river was gouged in the earth, the embankments on each side rising nearly twenty feet.

The sky quickly turned velvet black.

Suddenly there was a vivid flash, and sparkles of stars with blue and red cosmic dust appeared over his head.

Then he opened his eyes and awoke instantly back in his bed.

He was able to recall most of the events of the dream quite vividly. He initially thought it was just another bad dream that he could brush off like no big deal, but almost immediately he noticed something was wrong.

"My throat," he croaked. "Something is stuck in my throat!"

Sure enough when he awoke he found himself having a raspy, steel wool feeling in his throat.

"It isn't possible! I was dreaming.. Wasn't I?"

He sat up in his bed. He tried to cough. He tried to spit. Nothing made a difference. He looked at his pillow and noticed some stuffing and lint particles had escaped through a small tear. "Did I inhale some of this crap when I was sleeping? Yes, that must be it."

But it wasn't. Orion had been cursed by the blue pills. The curse they contained was able to attach to his astral body and partially return to his physical body in the Real, resulting in a terrible infection.

Later that day, Orion's symptoms had worsened. It could not have possibly been a piece of lint he accidentally inhaled off of his pillow, he confessed. He appeared to be full blown sick. He had a nasty sore throat and it felt as though there was a piece of sandpaper stuck in his trachea. "I can't believe this. I didn't feel sick yesterday. That dream! Damn it! That vile lady! It's as if those pills really did get caught in my throat! I don't understand this.."

There was nothing he could do.

The next day he felt no better, but at least didn't feel any worse. It had seemed that this was going to have to run its course just like any other cold.

In the early afternoon, his cellphone began buzzing.

"A call! Maybe this is about the job!"

He picked up the phone and answered as clearly as he

could with his sore throat.

"Hello?"

"Hello," replied a woman's voice. "My name is Stacey. I'm calling from the Department of Corrections. I was hoping to speak with Orion Brown," she said.

He replied in his dry cracking voice, "yes, this is he, how may I help you?"

"I have good news, Mr. Brown. We would like to consider you for the position. I was wondering if you would be available next Monday for a final interview with the Chief Commissioner."

Orion's sudden excitement turned to an anxious concern.

"Yes, well erm.. Unfortunately I have come down with some sort of flu. Monday you said?" He paused. "Today is Wednesday," he thought. "That should be plenty of time to recover." Before Stacey could reply, Orion said boldly, "I would love to come in on Monday for a second interview. I am certain I will be well by then."

"Ok, Mr. Brown, that sounds fantastic! We will see you then. Have a nice day."

As Orion put the phone down a troubled look came upon his face. "That gives me five days to recover," he said, reassuring himself. "That should be plenty of time."

The next day when he awoke, he no longer felt sick. Relieved, he began his morning routine. After his cup of coffee his mother called. But when he answered, he had no voice.

"You have got to be kidding me!" he thought. He hung up the phone and sent a message to her explaining he must have laryngitis. So much for being in the clear.

By Sunday, he was able to speak again but his voice sounded hideous. He sounded like Popeye, but worse, raspier and deeper, and more constrained. It was as if he had smoked two packs of cigarettes at once. It was too late to reschedule the interview, he thought, and if he had, surely they would have hired a different candidate. Calling out sick for a job interview couldn't possibly be a good way to convince an employer of one's reliability.

On the day of his interview, he tried not to worry. "They had already interviewed me once before," he said to himself. "They already spoke to me on the phone. They must know my voice doesn't normally sound like this, maybe they'll understand and it won't make a difference in their decision."

But those guys hardly mattered. It was all up to the Chief.

When he was called into the Chief's office upstairs of the building he first interviewed, he introduced himself, and briefly explained that he had laryngitis and lost his voice.

But the commissioner seemed off put immediately, and perhaps slightly suspicious of Orion.

"Oh, God, he must think that I am huffing paint to sound like this," he thought.

He summoned as much confidence as he could, and he proceeded to answer the commissioner's questions to the best of his ability. It seemed to be going well until he stumbled on one question however, where he confused the word "instigate" with "intimidate" when touching upon the topic of working amongst the prisoners. He hoped it wouldn't make a difference.

When he left the office, he could see there was already another candidate waiting for what must have been his second interview, too. He was a massive, lunk head looking guy, wasn't even wearing a suit or dress shirt, but cargo shorts and a t-shirt.

"Man, they definitely won't hire him," Orion said. But that guy looked like the perfect jarhead that belonged working in a prison. Perhaps he was retired military, and dressed so casually for his job interview because he was really that confident.

Feeling defeated, Orion drove home rather slowly, sulking.

The next day, his voice started to return to normal. He wasn't too pleased. He was suspicious if there was someone, or something messing with him. At least he hadn't any more nightmares with that wretched, evil succubus demon, or whatever it was.

Two months later the DOC finally sent him a letter with their "sincerest apologies" but another more qualified candidate was chosen.

The rejection burned him for a while, but later in life he would discover there were better opportunities in store for him all along.

The Lord had never abandoned him.

Christ continued to spectate the events taking place within Orion's mind, waiting patiently for him to remember.

CH. 3

Lucid

It would be one more year before Orion's genetically mutated DNA sequence would finally succeed in updating his living code to counteract and fully neutralize the dark matter in which he had been poisoned by.

The System was unsuccessful in its attempt to disable him after all.

Although his progress was greatly hindered, he was now on the verge of unlocking his ability to astral travel again. He would lucid dream nearly every night, and on a few occasions even managed to leave his physical body while remaining self aware.

At first he could only float several feet above his sleeping body before glancing back at himself, becoming startled and waking up. On his next attempt he made it through the ceiling but got stuck in the attic. By the following week he managed to float completely through his roof and into the night sky, making it as far as halfway down the street before waking back up. But this was only scratching the surface. He desired to journey to The Other Side, the place he could have sworn he had been a visitor of before; a place where he could visit magnificent worlds and places via the supposed "astral plane."

Some of his memories from before the attack had returned to him, and although he did come to some understanding of what had happened to him, it was still an enigma. The difference between past memories of dreams and past memories of reality was difficult to decipher. What he did know was that without witnessing the "white light at the end of the tunnel" or experiencing intense full body vibrations, he likely hadn't left the 3rd dimension.

The white light at the end of the tunnel mesmerized him. Maybe heaven was located there, he thought. Or perhaps, beings of a higher consciousness waiting to greet him and gift him with some enhancements to his life! How could he settle for living a traditional life on Earth while the beautiful mysterious patterns of the stars waved to him from the night sky above? He felt separated from something that he was supposed to be a part of; something he was once a part of.

He decided it was time to take his training to the next level.

Once he was able to "wake up" in a dream again without physically waking, the hardest skill to remaster was learning how to move around and change the scenery without getting startled, especially when flying. To engage in motion without any concern of gravity defied the laws of physics that he was used to. Of course, the laws of physics are absent in astral projection, except those which the participant believes and agrees to exist, so not only did he have to learn how to remain focused in this state, he had to unlearn the rules of reality, bypassing his subconscious logic. Otherwise, his abilities would remain limited to what he believed them to be in the Real.

He found himself standing on the corner of Princeton Road where the train bridge crossed overhead, about a half mile before the Route 2 East and Westbound highway ramps were located. His old neighborhood and the PLT were just down the road in the opposite direction. It was a pleasant late spring day, with light blue skies and large cumulonimbus clouds. A comfortable breeze passed through him, gently caressing the bright green foliage.

He began walking under the bridge, checking to see if there was any oncoming traffic around the corner. He felt that he was moving too slow, and should hurry up.

He thought of a bicycle, and instantly he was pedaling on a red bicycle picking up speed.

He passed under the bridge and continued up the road as it stretched out before the highway. A car passed him in the opposite lane, and he noticed another car was approaching behind him.

Now beginning to feel rushed, he turned his attention to the sky, and immediately began floating upwards, still on the bicycle. He managed to float about forty or fifty feet in the air, making quite the distance before he couldn't help but to expect the resistance of gravity pulling him down. He tried to fight against it and pedaled harder, but he slowly sank back down to the asphalt.

The feeling was most strange. He felt no wind in his descent back to the ground. His body had become weightless. Although he was startled by the delayed onset of gravity, he did not crash or injure himself. He was now fully aware that he was in a dream and could not fight the reflex of waking.

Then, as quickly as it started, his astral tether pulled his consciousness back to his body from the Astral Mezzanine, and he woke up once again safely in his bedroom.

A few days later he dreamt he was at a country fair. It was late at night, and there were crowds of people and colorful lights everywhere. He stumbled upon a little shop that oddly seemed to resemble the mini mart down the street from Sadie's old house.

He walked in, glanced briefly at the aisles of snacks and drinks, then noticed a row of bright yellow whoopee cushions hanging from a display rack. Nostalgic to his childhood, he had to have one. He paid the cashier and returned outside to the fair.

No one had seemed to notice him yet, and he hadn't particularly recognized anyone either. He excitedly tore the whoopee cushion from the package and began inflating it.

Suddenly it turned into a small hot air balloon, and it seated him in a chair-sized basket.

Within moments, he had risen at least eighty feet into the air, looking down at the crowd, taking in the lights of the ferris wheel in the distance. It was then, he realized he was dreaming.

"I've been waiting for this. I can do this."

He looked down, watching as he continued to float towards the right. He was unable to go any higher or lower, so he remained drifting in the air at neither a slow or fast pace.

A few moments later he was already at the edge of the fair, approaching the dark downtown buildings and roads.

"Ok," he said. "I want to get down now."

It took a few tries, but he slowly managed to float back down to the ground.

A moment later he realized he was standing in front of the strange shop he had purchased the balloon from. Sadie was there, waiting for him. He could not remember what was spoken. The rest became a blur.

The next morning when he awoke he was able to vividly recall the magical balloon and the excitement of flying. It appeared that he had to use some aspect of logic for his subconscious mind to cooperate in the experience, hence why he was more successful in flight on a balloon than he was on a bicycle.

It was a beautiful day with a cloudless deep blue sky. Patchy fields with evergreen trees stretched far and wide. The colors were wonderfully vivid, and he could feel a warm tingling sensation at his core.

He was happy.

He decided to waste no time.

He made a vigorous leap upwards and within seconds he was already hundreds of feet in the air. He scanned the view below. It appeared to be a wealthy suburban town, possibly Colorado, with rows of spacious homes and plush green lawns. The town was oddly flat and perfectly square, with a series of tall mountains in the distance.

Then, his subconscious mind began to remember logic.

After a few moments he could not ignore the obvious. Orion fell swiftly to the ground, yet landed gently, and uninjured.

He realized he was dreaming and felt himself beginning to wake up.

"No!" he shouted. "I want to stay here!"

He calmed his breathing.

"I must relax," he thought. "Concentrate."

He had a creative idea.

"I want an airplane!" he shouted.

Suddenly, a tiny blue jet plane appeared in front of him. He focused on the plane and before he knew it, he was already inside the cockpit. The engines were fired up and ready to go.

"Ok, now I need to find a runway," he said.

There was a narrow grassy stretch within the field before him, but it didn't seem like it was quite long enough. Alas, it was the best he could come up with, so it would have to do. He did not know how to fly a plane, but that didn't matter here. He just had to feel it.

Sure enough, he began accelerating.

However, when he reached about twenty-five miles an hour or so, the plane seemed to top out.

Not fast enough.

He was running out of space and would soon crash into a section of trees.

"C'mon, c'mon! Faster! FASTER!" he shouted, and the plane thrusted with a great surge of speed and began to take flight.

He pulled on the yoke with both hands as hard as he could and he continued to lift higher and higher until he cleared the trees at the end of the runway by a sliver, continuing to gain altitude until he could see the entire landscape below him again. No skyscrapers or highways, just homes and residential roads. The mountains that encompassed the valley were too tall to see over.

He zoomed and swooped through the sky for a good while, then decided he wanted more. Perhaps he could soar beyond the boundaries of the snow peaked mountains. He turned towards them at full speed, but as he approached the perimeter he was still not high enough to clear them. He tried to pull the yoke again and turn the nose of the plane upwards, but it wasn't moving. The mountains were getting closer, and the blue sky was disappearing from view.

Despite his efforts, he was actually now sinking.

No matter how hard he tried, he could not get the plane to rise any higher. Determined to not let the experience end, he decided to try turning around and go somewhere else.

As soon as he changed the direction of the plane, he effortlessly regained control of it.

It appeared the mountains were the limits set by his mind.

After some more intense flying and g-force, his excitement began to wear off and he started feeling slightly uncomfortable.

"Okay, I'm done," he proclaimed, and he decided it was time to revisit the ground.

However, similar to when he attempted to surpass the perimeter of mountains, he began to have difficulty controlling the plane again. He managed to slow down and descend to ground level, but the response from the plane was becoming sluggish. He found his makeshift runway in the field but despite braking as hard as he could, the plane would not touch the ground or come to a complete stop.

Feeling himself beginning to wake up, and unable to fight it any longer, Orion shouted, "to hell with this then!" and let himself crash into the trees.

Immediately his eyes shot open and he was wide awake in his bed.

He was astonished.

He closed his eyes again and replayed the experience over and over again in his head.

"Maybe I was straining too hard," he thought. He recalled that when he was struggling to control the plane he was holding his breath and tensing up the muscles in his body as hard as he possibly could. "Maybe I need to work more on letting things play out in faith instead of trying to force it to happen."

To override one's sense of logic, while simultaneously operating in relentless unwavering faith, took a lot of practice and constant effort, or so he thought.

It was a dark and stormy night. He was traveling down a long, empty desert highway in the back seat of an extended cab truck, a Dodge Ram, like the one his father used to drive on their way home from their summer fishing trips. Although this was not his father's truck, it felt strikingly similar. He sat behind the driver; as for who was driving was uncertain. He popped open the cab window, letting a cool breeze flow over his face as he peered out at the sky, just like he used to when he was a boy.

He was stricken with awe from the scene taking place before him.

A massive lightning storm had suddenly erupted over the desert sky.

The loud bursts, cracks and booms of the lightning fascinated him. The bright white electric veins turned the surrounding black sky to an eerie bruised purple with each flash.

For a moment it was comforting, reminding him of the evening thunderstorms that would light up the sky on those drives back home from the ocean.

However the comfort was not to last.

There was something peculiar about this storm. There were no clouds. He could smell rain in the air and could hear the droplets hitting the truck, yet everything was dry.

Another vein of lightning flashed and the sky changed. The stars began to reveal themselves with such clarity and detail it was as if he was looking directly into space.

He still had no idea he was dreaming.

Then it happened.

With a **BOOM** shaking his chest followed by a blinding flash, two explosions of light appeared in the middle of the night sky. Then, after only a second, there was another BANG and the two white lights shot across sky westbound, leaving perfectly parallel glowing streaks behind them, staining the horizon. Blue and red sparkling clouds of cosmic dust began to surround them, further enhancing the beauty and horror of this event.

It was as if a hole into outer space had quite literally formed in the sky.

He felt excited yet terrified. He realized this was no peaceful drive home.

They were running for their lives.

The truck sped up, and he still couldn't make out the driver. He returned his gaze to the window. There was something so profound about the spectacle taking place, he had to see it. He was too intrigued to care about his safety. He wanted to be closer.

The glowing white streaks of light and clouds of cosmic gas remained, as if the fabrics of time and space had been torn and disturbed.

Suddenly the sky turned to daylight and all evidence of the grand event had vanished.

The truck pulled over off the road and parked in the dirt, making a cloud of reddish-brown dust. As the dust cleared, a freshly paved tarmac runway revealed itself, and a jumbo jet alongside with it, surrounded by golden-pink clouds. He dashed for the jet without a second thought. He never did notice his driver.

Despite being a massive passenger jet, Orion entered by walking up a small staircase through retractable doors, as if it were a school bus. A stewardess dressed in blue asked for his ticket. He reached into his left pocket and sure enough, the ticket was there. Even more odd, the plane was already filled with passengers. The cockpit was open for all to see; there were no doors or curtains separating it from the passengers who were seated on brown bench seats without belts, further resembling an old school bus.

It was then he realized that *he* was the pilot, and the passengers were waiting for him. He jumped in the cockpit and hastily accelerated down the runway, this time hardly touching any controls, his subconscious mind not yet challenging the absence of logic. He was able to just *feel* the jet and control its movement by will. With a burst of confidence and concentration, he commanded the jet to soar upwards, and they were airborne.

He realized he was dreaming now, but embraced it, and took complete charge of the experience. He stayed focused on flying and did not have fear, although he was mesmerized. Maneuvering this jumbo jet was much different than the mini jet in the suburban mountain valley. The power and velocity was much more aggressive, the ascent into the sky was intoxicating. He felt nearly mad with power. He did not know where he was going, he just wanted to keep going up. Although the jet responded to his maneuvers much quicker and with more obedience than it ever could in the Real, when he tried to shoot it straight upwards like a rocket he was unsuccessful. So he continued riding it like a roller coaster, making dips and rises to gain momentum, then zig-zagging back and forth upwards higher and higher.

He embraced the tingling sensation in his core at each

free falling dip, and the sensation of his face being dragged to the floor from the g-force of being propelled back upwards. He felt one with the fuselage. It was as if it was his own energy that carried him, and the jet was simply a disguise.

The poofy golden pink clouds took up nearly the entire sky, with rays of light permeating through. He was now satisfied, and the jet became motionless.

He was here. Orion stood up and went for the door.

"Hey, where exactly do you think you're going? I was supposed to be in Cancun three hours ago!" shouted one of the male passengers.

"Cancun?" chimed in a female passenger. "I thought we were going to Kentucky!"

Orion turned to reply, but the passengers suddenly vanished. The school bus door was wide open. He made his way off the plane and stepped barefoot on the clouds. They felt soft and cool, and supported his weight.

He looked back and the jet disappeared.

The clouds had connected together, forming the entire landscape. There was no visible drop beneath him. The clouds formed the ground under his feet. The floor of clouds connected to a walled walkway before him, also made of clouds. He decided to follow it. The walls were just over his head so he could not see over them. Above him the sky was a misty pink.

After a few moments of walking, the cloud walkway ended before a strange structure that resembled an ancient Greek monument, with marble steps and tall white pillars.

Orion continued to the platform.

The marble steps were so smooth that they felt wet on his bare feet. As he entered the structure, he saw there was a woman inside. She was wearing a purple silk robe, flowing ever so gently over her mid-section. Her back was still facing him. She turned around, smiling, and gazed into his eyes. She appeared to be of Indian descent, dark cacao skin and silky black hair, yet her eyes were blue. Neither Orion or the woman spoke. She continued to smile and pointed to the end of the platform, motioning him to go.

As he approached the edge of the platform, the marble floor began to feel warmer and warmer until his feet tickled, creating a prickling sensation traveling up his legs.

He peered over the side.

The ground of clouds had disappeared. Instead, there was a jaw dropping fall into a cyclone of cloudy gray mist, with a strange green hue at the center. He turned back to ask the woman if he was really supposed to jump, but she was gone. The tickling sensation was now turning into an immense vibration, going up his legs into his torso. The strange prickling and tickling was becoming too much to bear. There was no time to ponder on the possible dangers of falling back to the Earth.

He had to jump.

He began to freefall so fast it felt like his body was being stretched through a rolling pin, but he embraced it. The whole experience was just too beautiful to have fear. In a state of bliss and awe, he continued to fall into the strange green center of the dark cloudy mist. When he hit the center, there was a massive, thunderous **BOOM** and **CRACK** like he had broken something upon impact.

Orion immediately lost all awareness and recollection of what had happened previously and was suddenly soaring through the sky at an unbelievable rate of speed.

He did not know it yet, but the traveling explosion of light that he had seen in the desert storm was him. It was he traveling so fast, he bent the fabrics of time and space, and saw himself doing it, before actually doing it. There appeared to be two streaks of light because he had crossed from the third dimension to the fourth; existing in two or more places at the same time.

He had done it. He had broken through to the Astral Plane, and in doing so had attained a permanently altered level of consciousness. He had taken "the scenic route" to the Great White Light this time, through a dream turning lucid-then turning astral; gradually elevating himself into the next dimension in stages.

It was incredible.

He separated from all awareness of past self and memories from the Real. He was only in the present moment. There was no longer a need for a plane, balloon, or any shred of complimenting logic. He felt as if he was still in his body, but he could not see his hands or arms. He soared through the horizon at what had to have been thousands of miles an hour.

He approached mountain ranges, lakes and forests, and passed over them in mere seconds. He was no longer confined by his third dimensional body. It was as if he was hundreds of miles wide, viewing the entire hemisphere of the Earth in all angles as he continued to soar through the sky like a rocket ship.

He had no set direction, or destination. There was no need, for he had no desire other than continuing to embrace the sensation of it all. He felt like he was flying in a superhero pose but his body was simply not there. He could hear and feel the wind whooshing and blasting by him, but nothing like what would be happening if he was actually in his body. At that speed, his flesh would be ripped to shreds.

He had become a traveling body of pure consciousness, with an ability to infinitely spectate and perceive his surroundings in any desired direction or location without having to turn his head, blink his eyes, or move at all for that matter. He did not have to leave the Earth, per se, to cross into the fourth dimension. The fourth dimension had always been there, coexisting across the entire universe. This is why beings in the fourth dimension can spectate the third dimension, but beings in the third can not spectate the fourth.

Time was difficult to measure in this state. It could have been a minute, or perhaps several hours that Orion continued to soar across the Earth before he decided to change his scenery. With his confidence and power at a new level, he felt he was ready to leave the Earth entirely.

Instantaneously he changed his direction upwards at full force, and left the atmosphere, entering outer space in a blink of an eye. He shot himself upwards with so much velocity that within moments he was already hovering over another strange blue planet that looked like Neptune or Uranus. He hadn't even noticed passing by Mars, Jupiter or Saturn.

Something about this planet was most fascinating to him. He felt a mysterious energy emitting from it, a feeling similar to that of being a lost child in the wilderness at night, although he was curious and filled with excitement. It was an eerie planet. It had different shades of blue to dark blue running parallel to each other. The stripes of color seemed to form grooves in the atmosphere, and they also appeared to be moving.

The planet was alive.

In the physical realm, Neptune was a frozen gas giant, but that wasn't the case here. Planets that appear desolate and lifeless in the third dimension may be lush and prosperous in the fourth.

He was overcome by a desire to swim and felt the presence of flowing waters here, so he dove into the planet head first, as if there was an olympic diving board in outer space, and the entire planet was the pool.

He quickly penetrated the atmosphere. There was no separation of sky or clouds. The sky was a seemingly endless overcast periwinkle mist composed of ice particles. He could feel that the air was cool, but the cold did not bring him discomfort, nor did the icy shards injure him. After free falling for quite some time, he still had not broken through the strange sky or reached any surface.

With only a little concern, he increased his speed rapidly.

A split second later he finally broke through the upper atmosphere and he could see below him. The planet was entirely covered in dark, purple-blue water. There were no visible land masses or mountains, only an endless dark ocean of nothing.

Orion plunged full speed into the dark cold ocean. The cool water flowing over him felt unusual yet divine. He swam back to the surface and observed his surroundings. There were no waves. The water was completely still. There didn't seem to be anything here, and the water was so deep he could not touch the bottom.

Suddenly Orion began to feel some of his human emotions returning to him. He felt slightly lost, as if he was far from home, deep in the woods during a cold thunderstorm, with the possibility of danger around the corner.

He was not ready for this experience to end.

He quickly cast aside his suspicious thoughts and reignited his explosive limitless energy.

He wanted waves, and he wanted big ones. He began raising a massive wall of water miles in height and width, changing the surface of the entire planet, sculpting it into a wave. He soared on top of the wave, pulling it higher and higher until he was nearly back in outer space again.

Now it was time to let the wave fall.

He belly flopped on the crest of the wave and intended to ride it all the way down. He dropped the wave and began the astronomical surf back down to sea level.

But something was wrong.

He was losing control.

He was going too fast.

He was free falling faster and faster and the wave was crashing down behind him. He was unfazed by gravity earlier, it simply did not apply to him unless he chose it to. But as quickly as his powers came, they were suddenly gone, and he was helplessly caught in a mega tsunami of his own creation, falling faster and faster down to what would surely be his death. He began to panic. He was surely going to die.

And just like that, Orion's astral tether snapped him back to his physical body and he awoke back in his bed on Earth, in the Real.

The Astral Projection was over.

Orion laid motionless in his bed for several minutes, absolutely mind blown. He could see that the sun had risen. It was probably about 7 AM. He usually slept with an eye mask, so the morning sun wouldn't wake him prematurely while he was still dreaming. He couldn't find the mask so he grabbed a pillow case and stuffed it over his eyes, attempting to fall back asleep again so he could go back.

But he couldn't.

He could recall most vividly the sonic boom of the lights as they streaked across the sky, and the sensation of soaring full speed through the atmosphere.

"It's as if I could see hundreds of miles wide, in all directions all at once!" he marveled to himself, still trying to comprehend it all. "Now seeing with my plain old normal eyes again feels like I'm viewing the world through a blurry glass! That sensation of being so close to the stars- and flying effortlessly through space.. But for what and why? Is this all in my imagination or is there really some greater spectrum of life out there?"

He racked his brain for answers, but it was an enigma.

He slowly raised himself out of bed and went downstairs to make his coffee.

CH. 4

Return to Jostania

By the time Orion was thirty years old, the factory and smokestack had been long torn down. Eventually it was condemned by the state for asbestos contamination and vandalism. The trail had re-opened, but it hardly mattered. Orion and his friends were usually too busy to hang out at the PLT like the old days. The high speed commuter rail expanded its service to the new Monchusett Station and frequently passed by on the old train tracks over fifty miles an hour, making the nostalgic walks to McDougal's too risky to attempt again even if they had the time. The good old days; the era of curiosity, romance and wonder from his youth, had come and gone.

What he did have now was his own luxury apartment, two cars and three jobs, but not without a cost to his health. After many failed attempts to return to the astral plane, he abandoned further pursuit of The Other Side and began channeling most of his attention to the Real. He worked around the clock, unable to enter the long undisturbed rest necessary to achieve an astral experience.

Oftentimes he wondered if the whole "Astral Projection thing" really even mattered. Now everybody was posting on social media platforms such as YouScreen, FacePage and Zweeter claiming to have out of body experiences like he had. Nowadays *everyone* thought they had discovered the secret of life, and couldn't shut up about it. And still, no one could really prove anything!

He felt foolish for thinking he was anything special.

It turned out to all be in his head.

Right?

Maybe the real world wasn't so bad and there was no such thing as some entity deliberately trying to limit the quality of his life, he assured himself. What good was dreamland anyway? He had died on numerous occasions in those lucid dreams, many instances of which were rather terrifying. He had even once narrowly escaped the bowels of Hell! Or so he imagined, that is. Furthermore, regardless of what he experienced in those dreams- regardless if they were real or not- he would always still return to reality afterwards like nothing happened.

"How useful did any of those out of body experiences prove to be?" he would question. "This Real world is inescapable, and by far more important. Might as well just make the best of it. It's time to grow up."

He dismissed any further thoughts on it. It was all a fantasy, probably lingering effects of all the psychedelic drugs he had taken with Gil in his younger days. He found a new appreciation in waking up soundly in his bed every morning, still alive, with his friends, family, pets and familiar things. Perhaps these were the greatest blessings all along.

Alas, nothing could compare to the joy of the good old days, when he had his first girlfriend, his first motorcycle- his first lucid dreams, the adventures at the PLT- Those were the times he missed more than anything. Not even another astral projection across the solar system could top that.

His love life had been rather dreary with the exception of a few spontaneous short lasting flings. His motorcycle had been long gone, and his guitar collected dust in the attic. As time went on, Orion continued to trade his health for an impressive paycheck, the pursuit of his dreams coming to a halt.

Little did he remember he was still the Universal Moderator according to prophecy.

He could only ignore his calling for so long.

One night, after a supper of beer and Chinese food, a most unexpected concoction to support another astral experience, it happened.

It was a pleasant summer day with a familiar scent of swampy river water and asphalt in the air. He stood on top of a grassy embankment next to a set of abandoned train tracks overgrown with weeds and shrubs. Tangled thorny overgrowth towered over his head. Pieces of the old track turned off onto an old concrete platform in front of him. He carefully pushed the thorny vines out of his way to avoid pricking himself, and went over for a closer look.

The platform had a rather odd, large drain cover in the center. He kneeled down by the cover and squinted his eyes. It had strange markings on it, looking like an alien language of some sort. Perplexed, he turned back and made his way through the brush and vines until he found the main tracks over the embankment.

They appeared to be the very same train tracks that he and his friends used to walk on during his teenage years; the same tracks that passed by the old abandoned steam plant!

He walked about a half mile down or so to see if the smokestack was still there.

Instead of coming across the faded gold brick smokestack he was expecting to see, there was a different, bizarre funnel shaped chimney in its place. Next to it appeared to be a small shed-like structure with a single window. Whatever else that used to be there had receded into the earth, leaving the sections of overgrown forest its place. There were no paper mills or power plants to be found.

He approached the small grassy slope off the side of the

tracks and lost his balance, sliding down to a flat section of overgrown weeds.

"Damn it!"

His blue jeans were stained with cool wet grass, and some spiky thistle stuck to his skin. He brushed himself off and stood up.

Suddenly a path appeared before him with twisted, tangled shrubs and downed power lines bordering the edges.

And it led directly to the mysterious upside down funnel shaped chimney.

At first it had looked about a hundred feet tall, and nearly a football field away.

But after getting a little closer it no longer appeared so large.

After following the path for another moment he was already face to face with the bizarre chimney. Vines protruded from the mortar of the bricks, wrapping and clinging around the funnel structure. It had to have been three stories tall at the most. The small shed-like building appeared to be a pump house, made of concrete, held up by rotting metal beams, with the door strangely left open.

Then he noticed a faint low humming sound.

"Was something still in operation here?" he thought. "Was there anyone here?"

Whatever purpose it had once served, it was now obsolete.

He became suspicious that the place wasn't real at all, and perhaps he was dreaming again. Yet, he was too intrigued to care. He had a strange tingling sensation in his palms, and a feeling like he might find lost treasure.

Suddenly his ears began to ring violently, followed by an abrupt muting silence.

He slapped the grippy, porous wall of bricks. There was no sound. He opened his mouth to speak. He could feel his voice vibrate but the sound was entirely absent. He wondered if he had a spontaneous bout of deafness. He stuck his pinky finger in his ear and sure enough heard the microphone tapping noise he was expecting. His ears were not the issue.

He turned around and noticed the sky was changing. A breeze swayed the tops of the long overgrown grass but didn't make any sound. Now that he thought of it, there were no birds or crows whistling either. He tried speaking again, but now he couldn't feel *or* hear his voice.

A pit of doom began to form in his stomach.

Something was wrong.

He changed his mind.

He wanted to leave. Now.

He was no longer interested in finding lost treasure. He realized he was dreaming and tried to wake up.

But he did not wake up.

"Oh no!" he said, still muted. "Is this real?"

He could remember his identity but could not remember his age or precisely which point in time he had come from.

He raised his right hand and touched the brick chimney again. A sharp burst of pain shot up from his palm and through his arm. Then the entire right side of his body felt like it was on fire.

In a panic, he ran to the open door of the pump house.

As soon as he stepped foot inside, a blinding white light engulfed him and he disappeared.

When he awoke, he had no idea how much time had passed. He couldn't remember a thing, and he did not know who he was. He only knew that he was cold and hungry.

It was dark outside. There were massive golden gates towering above him, connected to equally high golden walls that seemed to extend to infinity on either side.

Suddenly something grabbed him, and he was raised to his feet.

"*We've got him,*" a man said into some kind of futuristic

looking walkie talkie.

An insta-voice.

The gate began to open with a thunderous boom. Bright magnificent light poured out and the Traveler was blinded.

"Roger that," replied another voice. "Bring him in."

The Traveler lost consciousness again.

He awoke sitting in a wheelchair. It appeared he was in some sort of meeting room. There was a long artisanal carved wooden table with large matching wooden chairs; oddly with 90's style patterned fabric cushions.

"Nurse! It appears our visitor is awake. Bring him closer to the table, so we don't have to shout across the room," said a man with a white curled wig, sitting at the end of the table. He appeared to resemble one of the founding fathers. Behind the man stood six guards with blue-gray skin and reptile-like features. They were wearing royal blue uniforms and tall black polished hats, armed with miniature toy gun-like weapons. A woman with brown hair and blue eyes wearing white scrubs politely nodded back and pushed Orion's chair to the center of the table.

"Very good Lisa. We will take it from here, we will alert you via insta-voice if we require your assistance again. And remember, you are not to say a word of our visitor to anyone. What you have witnessed here today is highly classified."

"Yes Mayor Walsh," she said followed by a brief smile, and proceeded to exit the room.

"Where am I..." Orion croaked.

"Good sir, we welcome you to the city of Jostania!" declared the man in the wig. "However, we are very puzzled at your arrival, as there is no way you could have possibly survived outside of these walls."

Orion, still dizzy from the sedatives he was under, looked at the man who he would soon discover was the mayor of this strange land, and said nothing.

"We have scanned your DNA and found no relation to local family genetics on file," the mayor continued. "What we did find, however, is that your mRNA sequence appears to contain *Glecian* ancestry. As I am sure you are well aware, interbreeding with the Glecians has been outlawed since 2902. You wouldn't happen to be, I don't know, a member of the *Alliance* now, would you?"

Orion returned the mayor's glare with a puzzled, clueless look.

The Glecians were a humanoid race of people with blue-gray skin and fang-like teeth from the planet Gliese 581 C. They had merged cultures, interbred and exchanged various goods with the humans on Earth 581 C. That is, many years ago, before racism and prejudice against the hybrid children would trigger their 5th world war. How this came to be, however, is a different story for another time.

"No answer, have you? Well then, maybe you'll care to explain how carbon dating of your hair reveals you are over one thousand years old?!"

"Where am I?" Orion asked, oblivious to the mayor's question.

"Don't play dumb with me, boy. Rumors have it that the *Alliance* has been preparing an underground rebellion, and they are in possession of a quantum generator. Explain yourself! Who sent you? Are you a spy?"

Orion looked around the room. It was all so strange. He concluded he must have gotten drunk and forgotten he was at a dress up party of some sort. Maybe they were all actors and he was late to the rehearsal.

"What are the Glecians?" Orion asked.

"The Glecians are these hideous brutes standing right behind me of course," said the mayor cunningly.

"Hey, cut it out, will ya? I tried so hard to look nice today! Why does everyone make fun of the way I look?" said one of the guards, revealing himself to be the emotional one.

"Oh, I'm not talking about you Patrick. You look stunning today. I was more so referring to Henry, who still has goulash stains around his chops and neck collar."

Patrick blushed and Henry scoffed.

"Let us not get distracted! We are still waiting for your response, sir. What is your name, and where are you from?"

Orion's head was still pounding. He wasn't in the mood for drama class.

"I am from *A-mer-i-ca* buddy, and I am not *one thousand* years old! I am only.. I am.. Oh yeah, I'm fifteen this year. Wait.. I mean, twenty-five... No, wait... What did you guys give me?! My head hurts... I think I'm gonna be sick.."

The mayor looked shocked, as if he was expecting a different response.

"Dear God Switch, perhaps you were right... Perhaps he really is.. *"The Traveler."*

Orion's eyes opened wide and he sat up straight as an arrow in his chair. Hearing *"The Traveler"* reminded him of something.. But what?

A large man in a white lab coat holding a transparent clipboard spoke up from the corner of the room.

"We believe this is not the first time you have visited us, young Traveler. According to *The Prophecy,* you had visited this place before, many years ago."

A fascinated grin appeared on Orion's face. Aliens? Prophecy? Yeah, he was dreaming again. That must be it.

He decided to play along.

He cleared his throat. "-eh hehm.. Yes, it is I, *The Traveler* of which you speak of! It appears my space ship has crash landed, and I suffered a slight loss of memory. Please bear with me as I am still regaining my... bearings. What may I have the pleasure in doing for you all today?"

"I told you man!" exclaimed Dr. Switch. "He's the real deal!"

"Hold your horses Doctor. I know you are just as eager and excited as the rest of us at this rare phenomena, but you know we have a strict policy here in Jostania. Now that he is here, he can never leave."

The mayor got up from his chair and made his way over to a holographic display screen on the wall, speaking with his hands held behind his back.

"Besides, we only have trace information of "The Traveler" left behind in the damaged files of our forefathers. The Prophecy has been dismissed as folklore, a myth- until now. We can't be certain that it is really him-"

"Then who in the hell else could he be?" shouted Dr. Switch.

One of the guards raised his weapon and cast a stern glare at the doctor.

"Samuel, lower your voltage pistol. I will be the one to determine whether or not Switch is getting out of line," said the mayor. The guard, who was supposedly named Samuel, in his dark blue uniform and shiny black pope-style hat retreated back to the wall without saying a word, his face expressionless.

"Forgive me Mayor Walsh," said Dr. Switch, revealing his respect and lower ranking to the mayor.

Now, Mr. Traveler," the mayor resumed, "regardless if Dr. Switch is correct, you owe him a thank you at the very least. Uninvited guests to our city are typically euthanized. We can't afford another pandemic taking place from unknown diseases or pathogens outsiders may bring! But he *insisted* you had vital information to reveal, information that may take our society to a higher level of consciousness! So we decided to spare you. So then Traveler, is it really true you come from Earth 581 B, and your country was called, A-mer-i-ca you say?"

Orion turned green.

"... A- actually sir- Mayor sir, I was just playing along. I thought I was in a dream! I have no clue what's going on here. I- I wanna go home!" He started to burst into tears. "I think I'm gonna throw up.."

"It's just as I feared.." said Dr. Switch.

"It's just as you feared, what!?" demanded Mayor Walsh.

"*The System*," replied Dr. Switch gloomily.

Mayor Walsh stormed over to the doctor and ripped the clipboard out of hands, tearing up the papers he had attached to it.

"Enough with your nonsense! There is no such thing as some "AI virus" tearing through the cosmos! The Prophecy is invalid! If it were true, he would have arrived over one hundred years ago. He is clearly a member of the Alliance toying around with a quantum generator! He probably suffered a reaction and his comrades fled, leaving him alone at the gate. Something is rather suspicious in you and Dr. Sampson's relentless obsession with this boy... Is it just me or has the stench of TREASON entered the room?!"

Mayor Walsh suddenly turned violent and angry, and cast a vicious glare back to Orion.

"You boy, if you were really the *"Traveler"* this old fool thinks you are, wouldn't you have at least had the decency to notify us prior to your arrival! I say let's kill him. He's obviously just another test tube baby, a decoy staged by those damned fools in the Alliance. His comrades must have gotten cold feet and abandoned him at the gate, yes that's it! And perhaps you fools forged the test results, to manipulate me into sparing him! Dr. Switch, I have heard enough of your bogus prophecy! This System and the supposed "AI quantum virus" is a load of boloney and you know it, and if it were real, then surely someone had tampered with quantum technology and now we are all in danger!"

Orion tried to run but passed out and fell on the floor.

"Damn it Norville, if I am a fool don't take it out on the boy! Get him some water!" exclaimed Dr. Switch.

Mayor Walsh winced at the informality of being addressed by his first name.

"Nurse Lisa," he spoke into his insta-voice, "we require your assistance immediately!"

Norville had done it.
Over one hundred years had passed since his failed attempt

to murder his Uncle Sven.

It only took him three years after Sven's disappearance to overthrow his parents and their political party, taking over complete and total control of the Jostanian government. Using age reversing technology that was kept secret from the public, Norville was now one hundred and twenty years old, yet only appeared to be in his mid-fifties. He took advantage of his sustained youth to further manipulate the Jostanian public into believing he had been chosen by God, demanding to be praised and admired by the people. Sven Walsh, also known as Dr. Switch, was now one hundred and sixty-six, his prolonged lifespan the result of his own genetic enhancement and time spent in suspended animation.

"Water will do nothing. We already replenished his fluids in the hospital. I am keeping a close eye on you, Switch. Report to me on his status no later than 0600 tomorrow morning, you hear?"

Dr. Switch had remained gazing at Orion, nearly breaking his act.

"Do you copy, doctor?"

"Affirmative."

"Good."

Mayor Walsh and the guards exited the conference room on the seventh floor of the Jostanian city hall, leaving Orion limp and unconscious.

"Dear God, what have I done..." Dr. Switch muttered under his breath before Nurse Lisa and a lower ranking officer burst through the door with a stretcher.

Orion awoke six hours later strapped to an examination table at approximately 0200 EST, in the year 3000 on planet Earth 581 C. The sensation of acid burning his throat and deep hunger pains were too great to remain asleep. As his eyes opened and his vision returned, he could begin to make out a dimly lit room with dusty white tile flooring. There were various gadgets and medical equipment scattered around.

"Welcome to the future, Orion!" Dr. Switch exclaimed.

The Traveler did not yet remember his name, and was unaware that he was being spoken to. His vision was still coming in and out of focus. He realized that he was strapped down yet felt very little desire to break free. He did not feel much of anything as a matter of fact, nor had he any desire to question why.

"Listen boy, I don't have all day. If you are the Traveler that the angels speak of, I expect that deeper hidden strength within you to at least keep you awake."

"Wh-Where am I?" Orion asked.

"Well, where do you think you are?" replied Dr. Switch.

He had a very quirky and sarcastic personality. He was a wild looking man, with a head of long curly black hair that was balding, with strands of white and grey fraying in all directions. He wore large circle frame glasses and had a shaggy unshaven face. He was slightly heavy, and always seemed to be smirking.

"Well, to be honest I don't know," Orion said. "And I don't think it matters anyway. All I do know is that I feel defeated. I feel that whatever it was that I was supposed to be doing or seeking, I have failed. All I know is that I feel weak and powerless, and I am only here because I have been spared, or something of the sort."

"Don't be so gloomy, will ya? Try to concentrate. What is the last thing you remember before showing up here?"

"...I remember train tracks, and trees... And a gravel path I think. I can remember some other guys yelling at me, and I felt like I was in trouble. I don't know. I thought that I had escaped or something, but then there was this horrid, sharp piercing noise- and a blinding white light. Now I'm here."

The doctor looked puzzled and hesitated before making his response, like he was expecting a different answer.

"Mhmm.. Mhmm.. Orion, can you tell me what year it is?"

"Who is Orion? That's not my name. My name is.. My

name is…"

"Alright, time to stop beating around the bush, we must begin the procedure right away. I have to warn you Ori- I mean, sir, you must remain strapped down in case you suffer a reaction."

"Suffer a reaction? What do you mean "suffer a reaction?""

"Well, it is possible that you have experienced severe head trauma, and your memories may be altered or damaged. These kinds of mental gymnastics would drive an ordinary man into a self destructive state of panic and confusion, given the current circumstances."

He paused, expecting a response from Orion but he said nothing.

"-But if you are who I believe you are, you've already undergone intensive training and mental conditioning, as well as enhancement to your DNA and genetic profile, as it was right here one hundred years ago, or about twenty years ago in your time, that the angels brought you to me. I have waited my entire life for this opportunity. I've lost my family, my son, and forged an entirely new life in preparation for this very day, and I'm not going to let that bogus brainwashed nephew of mine ruin it. We the citizens of Jostania may be damned to live the remainder of our days robbed of our human authenticity, but that doesn't mean you have to. You may be mankind's only hope of a future without this hell, or possibly even prevent it from ever happening in the first place."

The words from the doctor passed through one of Orion's ears and out the other. He still showed no enthusiasm or interest. In fact, upon hearing this, his expression remained the same. He had no opinion or concern.

"Trust me kid, you're as good as dead if we don't do this. We have nothing to lose. Before we begin, let's get a few things straight. This is not the first time we've met. Your name *is* Orion, and you *are* the 445th Traveler. We live in neighboring alternate realities. The last time I saw you, you were just a boy."

Orion still could not digest or comprehend what this

crazy old doctor was talking about.

"The angels have gifted you with an extended life, and so have I. You might not understand how this is possible, but you are over one thousand years old, and I am one hundred and sixty-six. However, your body has appeared to have only aged about thirty years, and mine about seventy.

Puzzled, Orion thought, "did this guy just say he's one hundred and sixty-six years old?" oblivious to the statement that he himself was one thousand.

"Our version of Earth is at a different point in time than your Earth, about eight hundred years or so further along. Time does not pass congruently between our worlds. The angels brought you to me about one hundred years ago in my time, where we genetically enhanced you and altered your genetic code in accordance with The Prophecy."

"I need a cigarette," Orion said. And a drink. A STRONG drink."

"Ha! Good luck finding tobacco and alcohol in this place! Anyway, where was I? Yes, that's right.." He cleared his throat. "Err-hem, second off, well.. We could be interrupted at any moment by the guards that will soon be looking to put a bullet in my head."

"Why would they do that?" asked Orion.

"It means that I stole you from the examination room. They were about to kill you. Norville already knows too much about you and he is afraid of you."

Orion fell silent.

"Let's not waste any more time. I have to put you under. I will be placing your cranium into suspended animation so I can use a micro incision laser to cut you open and close you back up without losing more than a few drops of blood. Then I will send a small jolt of electricity through your central nervous system and attempt to re-sync the time crystals back to my Astral Scanner to retrieve your quantum memory.

"What kind of drugs are you on, man?" Orion chimed in.

"Don't be a wise ass," Dr. Switch snapped back.

"Ok, fine. Hurry up. Anything is better than staying stuck like this."

Dr. Switch hastily placed a gas mask over Orion's mouth and nose.

He immediately went to sleep.

Now was the time to act.

There was no room for error.

He quickly swiveled a strange pad-like machine over Orion's head, connected by a flexible wire attached to a table on wheels. It looked similar to a dental X-ray machine. He flipped the switch on the strange device and a purple beam of light flooded down, forming a square over his face and neck. Then he dashed for another larger machine mounted to a rolling desk, that had what appeared to be robotic arms controlled by a joystick. With the purple beam of light still encompassing Orion's head, Dr. Switch turned on the microsurgery machine, and with a few flicks of the joystick, an incision was made in Orion's skull behind his ear. His skin parted, yet no blood spilled.

Dr. Switch carefully pulled three glowing green crystal shards from a purple silk purse and placed them into a petri dish.

"Gorhan said to only use these in case of an emergency. I think it's safe to say this qualifies as such." He plucked each crystal up from the dish with a pair of tweezers and carefully placed them in the incision behind Orion's ear. He returned to the microsurgery machine, and pressed a small green button. With another light tap of the joystick, and a quick press of the small red button on the top of the handle, the machine sealed Orion's skin back up instantly. The beam of light turned green for twenty seconds and then began to fade.

It appeared that the procedure was complete.

Dr. Switch ripped the gas mask off of Orion and attempted to swiftly put the machines back in an orderly fashion.

Orion was breathing but still unconscious.

"Now time for the last step!" exclaimed the mad doctor.

He took what appeared to be an AED and connected the

electrodes to Orion's chest. With a quick jolt, Orion's eyes burst open. He took a loud gasp of air and aggressively jerked his chest up, the straps around his wrists quickly snapping him back. He let out an animal-like howl, panting and squirming ferociously.

"Orion! Boy! Focus. Take a breath. As soon as you calm down I can unstrap you. The bad guys aren't here yet, we still have time!"

Orion began slowing his breathing but not before breaking into a sweat.

"Now concentrate. Control your breathing. Everything will come back to you, but stay focused. Don't panic."

Orion jerked his head back and forth. He was trying not to panic but he could feel a sharp blade of terror in his core. He felt lost, trapped in something. Out of place. What was this place? As he began recollecting his wits he made eye contact with Dr. Switch and immediately froze, his eyes bulging.

"Wait a minute, what do you *mean* there's crystals inside my brain!?"

"WELL I'LL BE DAMNED, IT WORKED!" exclaimed Switch.

"I thought I was just dreaming! You're telling me I really am abducted by aliens? Why do you look human then?"

"Because I am human" If anything, you are the alien," replied the doctor cunningly.

"Untie me from this thing!," Orion insisted.

"Oh yes, where are my manners? It was only necessary for your procedure. Here, let's get you out of these."

Dr. Switch unclipped the straps and Orion tried to sit up immediately but he was too dizzy.

"Woah hold your horses man, it may be another five minutes before your anesthesia wears off." He quickly kneeled down and helped Orion on to a chair.

"I still don't understand what's going on."

"I wish there was time for the whole story, but all you need to know is that it was *I* who made this city. That shit head wig wearin' clown that calls himself Mayor is my nephew. My brother and whore sister in law were consumed by greed and they all turned against me, forcing me to fake my own death. Since then I've been incognito, under a new alias. The whole population is now under the Walsh family's reign, that is, the bad Walsh's. Damn them for ruining my good name. Although I must say I'm looking pretty good with this new face.."

Orion didn't laugh.

"-Ahehm, anyway, they are trying to turn everyone into clones! Brainwashed robots! Even brainwashing themselves in the process. What was once the greatest remaining utopia on Earth has turned into a madman's experiment! We aren't even allowed to drink soda anymore unless it's Saturday. How does that even make any sense? They've thrown people in prison for drinking any sweetened beverage outside the hours of -"

"Enough." Orion interrupted. "I've heard enough, just tell me what the plan is."

Dr. Switch looked perplexed. Now that he thought about it, he hardly had a plan. He didn't really think he would have made it this far. He had been rather expectant to have died by now.

"I figured if we made it this far, *you* would know what to do. Don't you have any powers? Legend has it you could move entire mountains with your right palm facing out."

"I don't know..." Orion sulked. I don't feel like I have any special powers at all."

"Well, maybe you just haven't remembered yet. Let's start small. Lift up your hand, and concentrate as hard as you can on the wall behind us collapsing. If you can move a concrete wall, you can move anything."

"...alright.. If you insist.. Here it goes.."

Orion lifted his hand and concentrated on the wall. He tried to imagine the wall blowing out like a ton of TNT was lit underneath it.

Nothing.

He strained harder, and harder and then-

Pffffffttt.

He farted.

Dr. Switch sighed. "We're doomed," he said.

Orion looked down at his feet gloomily.

"Well, I tried."

"There is one place, Orion, where you may be able to transcend from this shit hole and escape back to your home world. Dr. Sampson the third, he is a good man. Been working with me for some time now. He has a quantum generator. He may be able to program it to transit your light energy and consciousness back to its place of origin. It is only ninety-nine percent accurate however- you will likely land on your home planet.. But you could miss and land on the moon.. Or even the sun-"

Suddenly armed guard after guard burst into Dr. Switch's hidden operating room under the Jostanian East District Hospital. Unfortunately they had been on surveillance the entire time while Norville, now Mayor Walsh, watched them from a holographic screen in his penthouse office, laughing maniacally. He had already learned of Dr. Switch's true identity when Nelson, the ex-con mortician, squealed their entire plan after being caught for stealing the body from the morgue. He decided to play along, and to watch and see over the many long years what Sven was hiding up his sleeve.

"What took you idiots so long!" Norville bickered at the guards as they brought in Orion and Switch, shackled and chained.

"It is quite the feeling," Switch began, "to have an entire lifetime of work.. GO COMPLETELY TO SHIT IN THE BLINK OF AN EYE!"

"Boo-hoo! So the show is over! At least for you two that is," Mayor Walsh hastily replied. "GUARDS!"

"Yes, Sir!" responded a unison of eight or so men with bluish gray skin and strange armor.

"Take Switch to the Euthanization Chamber, and leave

the Traveler with me.

Orion started to panic. "I just want to go home! I hate this place! I–"

PINCH!

One of the meatier guards held Orion down and injected something behind his ear using a handheld device. Fortunately, the ear opposite to the one Switch had tampered with.

Orion stood up. "Actually.. This ain't too bad.." he said coolly. "I.. Actually.. Don't have any complaints at all as a matter of fact." He looked around the room, with a smirk on his face. "Hey, how's about I propose a deal to you all?"

The room fell silent. It appeared no one was quite expecting this reaction from him.

"You, the Quaker Oats lookin' guy. You say you're the one in charge around here?"

"That's Your Highness, to you, boy, but do go on with your proposal."

"Perhaps you might reconsider sparing my life. I belong to no alliance, nor do I have anything to do with this prophecy. I am very willing to join your society and work amongst your people. I have valuable knowledge and skills, it would be quite a shame not to utilize me."

"Oh, to hell with that Orion! Don't do it! Don't sell yourself out so easy, *Gorhan* and *Katiru* would never abandon us–"

"WHAT IS THIS SCUM STILL DOING NOT IN THE EUTHANIZATION CHAMBER?" Norville shouted.

"Right away, Sir!" barked back Henry, the largest of the guards, as he gripped the doctor behind his neck and dragged him out of the room.

The Mayor quickly regained his composure. "Oh, so it seems the personality enhancement chip is compatible with your blood type! Good call Henry, I would not have expected a PEC to work on him!"

"Just doin' my job, sir," Henry said as he bowed, basking in his opportunity to receive praise.

The mayor turned around with his hands behind his back and paused, thinking. A moment later, he cleared his throat and said, "We the citizens of Jostania would be honored to have you join and serve our community, in exchange for sparing your life. However, it is Jostanian law that you remain up to date on all your vaccinations, and retain your new Personality Enhancement Chip at all times."

"Boy I'd say! This really is a personality enhancement chip. I'm feeling better already!" Orion proclaimed.

"I fancy mine as well!" replied the mayor enthusiastically. "Sampson really knows his stuff. He is our lead scientist and engineer down at JIT, the Jostanian Institute of Technology. Or rather at least, he was, because when I find out what he's been doing with Switch behind my back all these years he's probably going to be demoted to a dishwasher. Since the breakthrough of PEC's, we have nearly eliminated mental illness from the population. A perfect sustained balance of dopamine and serotonin is achievable with this new technology, stimulating GABA to travel through semi permeable membranes within neuronal passageways within the brain at controlled intervals, allowing for humans to operate at their fullest potential without the need for drugs or over indulgence. We have quite literally cracked the scientific code for happiness."

Orion was rather impressed with the mayor's bit, but then heard Switch's words as they replayed to him in his head. *"They are trying to turn everyone into clones; brainwashed robots, even brainwashing themselves in the process."* But he felt rather enhanced since being implanted with that chip a minute ago. "Maybe it's not the end of the world afterall," he assured himself. "Maybe living here will even be fun."

Henry, with his oversized hands and fingers, pushed down too hard on the injection gun's nozzle when implanting Orion's new chip and damaged it. The chip was short circuiting in his brain, making him feel high and over confident.

"Samuel, please remove the Traveler's shackles and cuffs," the mayor said to the guard that had been present on their first encounter. "And escort him to the registry so he may receive an ID badge and job position. And someone bring me Sampson!"

◆ ◆ ◆

Dr. Switch had made it only halfway down the hall before Henry put his triple pronged stun gun through his eye socket. He died on impact, with blood and segments of brain oozing from his nostrils. His body was still and lifeless on the floor in a pool of blood when Orion and his escort stumbled across them.

"Damn it, Henry!" Samuel shouted. "The Boss is going to have us both for this, you fool!"

"He was going to kill him anyway, wasn't he? He called me a big dumb oaf, and said that my wife is a whore!"

Samuel sighed, putting his face into his hands.

"I'll deal with the body, you two get the hell out of here!"

Orion went back into shock and blacked out.

◆ ◆ ◆

"Sir, Sampson is in the lobby waiting to see you now," said a nasally voice through Norville's insta-voice.

"Good. Bring him in."

A middle aged man with blonde hair and a white lab coat burst through the double doors of Norville's penthouse suite.

"You son of a bitch, you better get on your hands and knees and pray that God saves you because I am sending you back to Hell!" snarled Dr. Eric Sampson III, staring down Norville in his eyes without blinking.

"You stupid baboon!" replied Norville. Did you really think I wouldn't have found out you were working for Sven behind my back! You better surrender the quantum generator before I have you imprisoned for life!"

"You will never find it! We have nearly unlocked the code to reset our entire timeline to before the war! We will not be stopped in restoring the world back to the way it should be!"

"We," huh? So there are more of you fools who wish to rot in the Jostanian prison cells? You know Sampson, I was going to offer you an opportunity to make amends. But I think I just changed my mind. Your quantum generator is probably just as useless as you are. Clearly this boy you all drummed up to be "The Traveler" of some long lost "prophecy" was a sham, and your first test subject didn't even make it past the gate without getting caught! Furthermore, your PEC updates are ineffective! We still have an underground movement of young adults questioning their reality and avoiding their vaccinations! I have no use for your half-assed technology and your pathetic dump of a lab anyway! I don't need you. You're RE-PLACE-ABLE."

Sampson was now suicidal. Moments prior he overheard on his insta-voice that his only remaining friend, Dr. Switch had been slain. He had genuinely put his heart and soul into his work, creating and restoring Jostanian devices for the government for years, without ever receiving proper credit or payment, and all this on top of losing his only son.

Anthony, who was only fourteen at the time yet already received a fully paid scholarship to JIT, had been caught on hidden surveillance cameras drinking soda apparently too close to the curfew hours. He was taken away in cuffs, screaming *"Dad! Help! Save me!"* as his fingernails gripped to their front door, peeling off in blood.

Norville had personally assured Sampson, who had also been arrested for attempting to fight off the officers as they dragged his son away, that he would have the charges dropped against them both on one condition. Anthony was to have alterations performed to his PEC, so he may develop increased obedience, as well as alterations to his gustatory cortex so he would lose his taste for sweetened beverages or foods. Furthermore, he was to complete his education at Cushing Academy, a boarding school that did not allow visitors. He assured him to have no worry, that it was still "a great honor" and that if he refused, he surely could have had him and his son sentenced to death.

Sampson knew that his son had been reduced to a vegetable, and the mayor was a psychopath. Anthony was as good as dead, and now that everything he had been working on with Dr. Switch had been exposed, he was ready to die himself.

Sampson did not delay. He immediately lunged for Norville and clasped his hands around his neck, squeezing as hard as he could. Norville choked, Samson's grip still tightening, the rage in his soul invigorating him. His body was in overdrive. Norville's eyes were fully open, popping out of his head. Sampson could see the look in his face, the look of shock and disbelief.

"Sampson, you dimwit. Sampson, you fool. I will have you killed. I will have you tortured. I will have your every limb slowly twisted and removed from your torso. I will pluck your eyes out with a fork and crush your testicles with a brick."

Sampson imagined Norville repeating those words to him once again, as they rang in his ears every day since he threatened to expose him after what he did to his son. This further enraged him. Sampson decided suffocating the corrupt Jostanian leader was not good enough. He wanted to feel his bones snap.

However, before he could finish twisting Norville's neck in a way it was never meant to rotate, the guards came rushing in and delivered a one thousand volt lethal shock to Sampson's spine. He died instantly, collapsing to the floor, releasing his grip from the corrupt mayor's throat.

Norville coughed and spat, groaning and moaning on all fours, being as dramatic as possible, although his breathing had returned to normal after only a few moments. The guards stood over him emotionless. Deep down they wish he had died.

◆ ◆ ◆

When Orion awoke, he remembered nothing. He only knew that he was far from home. It appeared he had been placed in some sort of motel, in a single small room with a toilet, fridge and a queen sized bed. There was a small pool outside, but the fence around it was chained and locked. It appeared to be summer and it was very hot. Outside he could see cars, roads, shops and a massive water tower. As a matter of fact, it looked like he had taken a time machine to the 1990's of his own world. There were 90's style cars and trucks, with sun blotched paint and rust. Otherwise it seemed like a typical day in an ordinary place.

On the small dresser beside his bed was an ID, an insta-voice, a credit card, and a note that said "ARRIVE @ 2000 N. Crescent St, 0800 SHARP."

It turned out Norville did honor his agreement to let Orion stay in Jostania, although he had never really intended to. However, considering the events that had unfolded the previous day, nearly losing his life and being humiliated, he felt the need to portray the image of a selfless leader seeking the greater good of his people. He needed assurance and praise from someone, anyone, to help heal his bruised ego. Alas, he enrolled Orion into the Jostanian society at a respectable middle class status, changing oil and replacing tires for military vehicles as they returned from their missions beyond the Dome.

Fortunately, after the complete and total disaster in the city hall building, he was so occupied with the press and covering up the murders of the two most reputable doctors in Jostania, the supposed "time crystals" in Orion's brain and the "Traveler files" left behind from his father and uncle were the least of his concerns. "Useless," Norville concluded to himself. "Make-believe magic rocks. Those morons probably really believed this kid traveled time and was from another planet. He was probably another test tube baby all along, and had his identity and memory erased. Yes, that's it. And then they planted him outside the gate.. Obviously got one of my worthless soldiers in their stupid "alliance"- all part of whatever master scheme they had to throw me off my rocker and strip me of power. "

There was still the dilemma, however, of the new

PEC's only having a lifespan of about two years without a lithium nano-particle shot, or what they labeled in Jostania as "vaccinations." With most lethal viruses having been eradicated during the nuclear holocaust, there was little need for real vaccinations anymore. But the less the public knew the better. Without his lead scientist Sampson, Norville also had about two years to figure out what he was going to do next in his societal experiments.

After several days, the effects of Orion's PEC began to wear off, but he decided to keep up the act as he plotted his escape. He praised the mayor, even speaking openly about his "selfless act of mercy" in allowing his stay. A few members of Sven's underground alliance had located Orion in secret, and explained to him that this was the place he had been transported to as a boy, and the strange experience previously thought to be just a night terror, was actually very real.

Apparently Sven, AKA Dr. Switch, implanted three small green crystal shards that were gifted from the angels into Orion's brain that allowed him to "merge between various frequencies at once, alter matter, and warp time and space" so his astral body could generate physical doppelgangers of his real body, coexisting in multiple realities simultaneously. He didn't really get it, but apparently the time crystals or stones or whatever they were called, were so powerful they were not only unable to be destroyed, but their harmonious frequency would overpowered his PEC anyway.

Orion, on the other hand, could see that the Alliance was still no match for the mayor and his army, so he decided to decline the invitation to join. He didn't care about the prophecy. He wanted to get the hell off their planet. He believed as long as he kept his cool, and stayed on the mayor's good side, he would find a way out in time.

He continued to work hard and conform to their society, and gained great respect and admiration within the Jostanian community. Knowing the power of the evil mayor, Orion took no chance at hinting his knowledge of the truth, and did his best to avoid further contact with the members of the Alliance, not daring to lose his status of declared competence and trustworthiness within the Jostanian military. He acted star struck every time Norville was around, knowing his flattery would soften him up as he prepared for the day that he would make his request.

By his two year anniversary of his arrival to Jostania, he was losing his will to live. The ten hour six day work weeks were hell. The soy bar diet, lack of romance and entertainment added insult to injury. He could not remember much from his life back home, he only knew he had to get back. This was a life not worth living any longer.

He arrived at the Jostanian City Hall in his worn down 90's style pickup truck with a six-pack of cherry Coke in glass bottles. The cost of the beverages, which had been preserved since before the war, had afforded him one year of vigorous saving. He knew he only had one shot at this, and he was going to do it right.

"Welcome, welcome Zebulon!" exclaimed Mayor Norville Walsh, as Orion entered the penthouse level of the City Hall.

His name had been changed to Zebulon. False memories to accompany his new identity had been downloaded to his PEC. Orion had been so successful in his act that Norville hadn't the slightest suspicion that his PEC had been defective all along, and the false memories had never taken root. He had been promoted to the highest ranking of military mechanics without any suspicion of divergency.

"Greetings, your Highness!" Orion, AKA Zebulon said charismatically. "I have come bearing gifts of *quayne!* Not just ordinary quayne, but VIP quayne, something I have been working hard for a long time to obtain."

Quayne was Jostanian slang for food, and VIP quayne was only permissible to the highest class.

"Cherry... COKE??" How did you get your hands on these?

Only Morticus of the West Region has these in stock, and I know for a fact they are quite pricey!"

Orion knew very well Norville could afford any tangible item in Jostania, but was too obsessed with his body image and maintaining public support of the Jostanian soy bar diet to ever be seen consuming a highly concentrated sugar. However, it was a Jostanian custom to always accept gifts from the lower class, and now Norville was marinating in anticipation, finally having an excuse to consume the tasty beverage without conflicting his ego or image.

"Yes indeed it is the real deal, please join me! I have also brought the finest Jostanian ice from the underground permafrost cellars, and crystal glasses made from the 24th century. Let us have a drink, as I have a special request I would like to make to your Highness."

Norville wasted no time, as if he had prepared his whole life for this particular day, and fetched a silk tablecloth and matching bibs from a locked drawer under his desk, one of which he handed to Orion. Orion laid out the precious decorative glass cups on the grand meeting table, and an insulated satchel containing the blue smokey ice. Using a golden scooping spoon, he placed the cubes delicately in each glass. He took the liberty of opening and pouring Norville's drink, which was a sign of respect to the higher class. The mayor watched with fascination as Orion tilted the glass to its side as he poured, avoiding the frothy over-foaming of the carbonated beverage. After he filled the cups, they both sat in silence. Orion knew what would be coming next and said nothing.

"Henry, you fool! Are you going to leave us sitting here like a couple of buffoons or are you going to retrieve sippy straws!"

Orion struggled not to burst out laughing, observing this man wearing a white curled wig, dressed like a French soldier from the Renaissance, demanding the curvy, spiral sippy straws like a child.

Here in Jostania, things were different. Alcohol was

banned, as it had a tendency to reduce the effectiveness of the citizen's PEC's although plenty was hoarded within the Walsh family and high ranking officers. Tobacco was a taboo, as most citizens of Jostanian descent had long lost the habit, so when ingested or smoked for the first time, the effect was considered undesirable, usually resulting in extreme nausea and headache for the user. The euphoria generated in consuming nicotine once a tolerance had been developed was only known to a select few, so by reason of low demand, tobacco was not regulated. Other forms of drugs, such as marijuana, had been long extinct since the war. Therefore, sugar was the most desired drug of Jostanian culture.

With the diet as bland and unpleasant as humanly possible, the special occasion of a soda pop would be the most euphoric, high generating sensation available to the public. This is why Henry the Glecian meat-head guard was so starstruck watching them reveal the bottles of cherry Coke, and forgot to bring forth the straws. He attempted to regain his composure but nearly tripped over his large clumsy feet as he bowed down and lifted a small golden briefcase over his head, presenting it to the mayor.

"Yes, erh-hem, good work Henry," said Norville, as he opened the case revealing transparent green and blue plastic crazy straws in velvet padding, one in a spiral, the other with loops like roller coaster tracks.

Henry retreated to the back of the room and bowed to show respect. A little saliva dripped from his jowls to the floor, fortunately without the mayor noticing. The cherry Coke was the center of attention in the room, and Orion noticed the other guards were also looking over them with strained eyes, like an old man seeing a young woman sunbathing in the nude.

Orion picked the blue loop straw, and the mayor selected the green spiral straw, and they both began to drink simultaneously. Norville had only taken a half a sip before throwing his head and hands back, moaning and groaning in pleasure.

"It's simply fabulous, truly a nectar of the gods!" he exclaimed, instantly high from the sugar.

Orion was blown away himself. It was the most delicious soda he had ever tasted in his life. The cola, sugar and cherry flavors danced on his tastebuds one by one. He was unsure if this soda was really that good or if this is simply what cherry Coke tastes like after two years of no sweets.

"I would like to obtain a Jostanian Exit Passport," he stated boldly.

Norville took his time formulating a response, going into thought. According to the story that he fabricated, "Zebulon," was born outside the gates of Jostania in a medical training camp. Zebulon's mother underwent special genetic therapy so the stem cells in her womb would be stimulated to become highly resistant to radiation, one hundred times greater than the ordinary human of that time, with his mother dying in the process of carrying a radioactive child. Her sacrifice for the enhancement of the human genome was to be the template for repopulating the planet. Norville thought he was a genius for coming up with the story. The only problem was, he had been under the impression that Orion's success in Jostania was simply the result of his PEC, which was due for an update soon, as with the entire population. Without Sampson, the new patch had never been completed.

"Not to worry, your Highness," the mayor's new lead scientist, Steve Harrison, had assured him. "For the common citizen has had a conditioned unaware mind for so long, the effects have likely permanently integrated within their minds with or without the chips."

Sure that might be the case for the general population, Norville had thought, but Zebulon is a wild card. If he starts becoming self aware, there's no telling what damage he may cause, especially with those damned members of the Alliance growing in number. He had assumed he would have no choice but to throw him in the incinerator, like he had intended for Sven. "Oh well, better him than me," he had concluded. "At least

I profited over two-hundred thousand *Cones* off this kid."

After loudly slurping and sucking down the rest of the sweet chilled bubbly nectar, and the guards nearly being reduced to tears of envy, Norville came to the conclusion that he was far too fond of this lad to throw him in the incinerator, and if he truly wanted to be released from Jostania, actually believing he was capable of surviving on his own beyond the gates, then as far as he was concerned it would allow him to terminate the boy guilt free.

After shooting the breeze and adding a bit more flattery to soften him, Mayor Walsh agreed to release Orion from the gates of Jostania. Orion opened the manilla folder with his citizen transfer paperwork and passport. Without hesitation the mayor used a blue stamp to press a triple triangle, macabre-like symbol (the Jostanian flag) on his passport and just like that he was legally freed from the prison of this man-made futuristic Hell.

Orion took one last look out of the window of the City Hall meeting room, taking in the strange New York city style streets and all the 80's and 90's styled cars. As it turned out, automobiles had never been manufactured beyond the 80's and 90's of this alternate reality, and of the available cars, there were only two colors, light blue and maroon, which were actually intended to specify the driver's gender.

Concluding his act and containing his excitement of being freed, Orion said in a closing statement to the Mayor: "In my thanks to having the wonderful privilege of serving the Jostanian community, and being awarded the highest ranking authority and trust to exit the Dome while retaining my citizenship in good standing, I would like to bestow the remainder of this VIP quayne to your Highness, for his most enjoyable and savory consumption. All I ask is that one of these sacred bottles be preserved for me, in the event of my successful return to Jostania, granted I survive beyond these walls."

Norville was thrilled. He couldn't believe the kid really thought he'd survive beyond the Dome. The remaining cherry

Cokes would surely be all his.

When Orion was released from the gate, he broke into a sprint and didn't look back even once. He continued on through the dry, barren stretch of land. He did not wish to ever see the place again as long as he lived. The sparkling golden walls were a lie. There was no prosperity in that city.

The supposed levels of radiation beyond the gates had actually been harmless to him, coincidental to Norville's completely fictitious story. For on Earth 581 B, cellular, radio and wireless internet communication devices had already generated high levels of radiation, which over time the general public had developed a natural immunity to, an immunity that no individuals in Jostania had retained. So he was as a matter of fact, actually immune. There were no werewolves, no hidden bombs or traps. No mutants or zombies. Just an open wasteland.

He decided to search for the strange funnel-like chimney that he had stumbled across before somehow teleporting here. Before long he found an old set of familiar train tracks. A few wild dogs ran past him but ignored him. He walked the tracks until he felt his knees weakening. He felt hot and cold at the same time. He felt hungry, yet his mouth was terribly dry. His mouth was so dry, in fact, it was all he could really feel. He became overwhelmed with a need to urinate, but even after going the sensation in his bladder could not be relieved. He decided that perhaps he would die here after all. He lied down and stared into the hot white sun. His vision began to blur and then turned black.

He awoke back in his bedroom on Earth 581 B.

He had returned to the Real. It was morning. It was all a dream.

His mouth was dry as a cement, and although he urinated in the dream, he managed to avoid soiling his bedding, and he quickly ran to the toilet to relieve himself. He looked at his reflection in the mirror, trying to process the experience. He felt rather disgusted, and shocked–absolutely flabbergasted at how he could have lived what felt like an entirely alternate life, and for quite some time, only to wake up once again realizing none of it was real.

Or was it?

The time crystals, the mad doctor.. The strange futuristic city.. He racked his brain. Why cherry Coke? And how did any of this correspond to the train tracks? Oh, hell with it, he thought. By now, he had been tantalized with experiences from The Other Side for the greater portion of his life. He had begun to accept this was just the way his life was, and there was nothing he could do about it, unless he wanted to end up in a crazy house. No one would or could understand. Being destined to fulfill some "angelic prophecy" was fictitious; an idea his over active imagination had come up with, he assured himself.

By the time he finished his coffee, all he could really remember was the Mayor's face, looking out of the City Hall window, and the image of the Jostanian flag stamped on his passport.

Everything else became a blur.

CH. 5

The Trip

ate would have it that the Traveler's physical body had grown too weak and embedded with toxins for the crystals to properly activate. Although the crystals were implanted in the astral duplicate of his body in a parallel reality, they would remain attached to him in all realities on a quantum level. The past year of working around the clock and neglecting his health had weakened his astral magnetic field. He had nearly forgotten of his trip to Jostania, and dismissed it as another crazy dream.

Fortunately however, Dr. Switch's last minute procedure on Orion was not in vain.

The time crystals, or the quantum generators, (not even Switch understood that he and Sampson's device was useless and the generator was actually in the form of the green stones all along) were only dampened in their effectiveness.

The transformation had still begun.

With his new surge of energy, Orion excelled quickly in his workplace and was transferred to a management position in Boston.

However, six months later the "new car smell" of his increased salary wore off. His promotion had proven to be a double edged sword, and was consuming him. Remaining trapped behind a desk all day and fighting bumper to bumper traffic was no longer worth the sacrifice of his available time and health. Now he desired to reclaim his health and fitness, and explore his lost talents and hobbies.

He left his position at the pharmaceutical company and started his own ecommerce business. He took temporary and part time jobs to fill in the gaps as he waited for his investments to grow. He downgraded to a studio apartment and sold his sports car, adapting to a lower budget lifestyle. He returned to the gym, and improved his diet and sleep. He began to have vivid and spectacular dreams again. He could feel the presence of something otherworldly returning to him.

He started to notice repeating numbers such as 444, then 222, first on the license plates of cars he passed, then branching out to the digits on clocks, receipts, bank statements, phone numbers and more.

He was not yet aware that these meant nothing.

But they triggered his awareness to something bigger.

He began to notice his thoughts reflected back in his reality. Sometimes a song he had been thinking of would just so happen to play a moment later on the radio, or in the background music as he walked through the grocery store. Sometimes he would be thinking of a person and shortly after they would coincidentally text or call him. Other times when he was thinking of a phrase or subject, he would hear it mentioned in the conversation of people he passed by moments later.

And that wasn't the all of it.

"The portal of the trees" as he used to call it, or the strange triangular pattern he noticed in the tree branches on the day he played hooky on his motorcycle as a teenager, had returned. He could not explain how or why, but he frequently noticed the familiar tilted half-cross outline of a distinct right angled isosceles triangle appearing in various places and things.

It was as if something was watching him.

The synchronizations, signs and wonders began to occur

so often he began to worry that he might be losing his mind. Something was trying to get his attention, and he was going to get to the bottom of it.

There was only one solution that he believed would clear his mind.

"Mom, this is really it this time. I've booked my flight, I'm going back to Hawaii."

"But what will you do about your cat? Your apartment? What will you do for a job?" she replied. "And what about me? I'll be worried sick about you."

"I know, don't worry. I'm only going to be away from May 1st to the 11th. It won't be like the time I lived out there for six months," said Orion.

"Thank God! It's far too dangerous out there! Haven't you seen the news about the volcanoes?"

Orion sighed. He already explained to his mother that there were no active volcanoes on Oahu. But it was no use.

"And don't you dare go swimming in the ocean alone!"

He gulped. Lately he had been having dreams of big waves, often frightening waves. Sometimes he would wake up in terror before the waves crashed on him, other times he managed to ride them to shore. Something about the ocean was calling to him again.

The flight was excruciating. He was so nervous the night before he only slept two hours at best. He scored a discounted ticket for the new direct flight from Boston to Honolulu, with an 0800 EST departure time, and 1400 HST expected arrival time.

This eliminated the layover that was typically in California or Arizona. He had been sure the nonstop flight would be better than taking a layover on the west coast, but it turned out to be much worse. Being trapped in economy seating for twelve hours straight was rather torturous. The seats were extremely uncomfortable with such little leg room and space to recline. The airline food was terrible. For reasons unknown, they served lettuce and tomato sandwiches with no meat. He was so starved by the time he arrived at the Daniel K. Inouye airport that he hardly had the strength to carry his luggage to the taxi pick up.

But after a few moments of stepping into the beautiful sun and warmth again, and having a smoke with a big local Hawaiian braddah by the bus stop, he caught a second wind.

By the chance of good fortune, his taxi came for him before a dozen others that had already been waiting at the same spot. The driver was a jovial rastafarian man. Orion shot the breeze with him, talking about driving gigs and the job market on the island.

"By the way," he said to the driver, "you don't happen to have any bud, do you?"

The man's face lit up. "Do I have buds? More like what kind do you want, braddah?"

Orion exchanged a twenty dollar tip for a small bag of pungent marijuana.

He arrived in Waikiki to pick up his rental car, and wasted no time as he navigated to the nearest Gual-Mart to get camping supplies and a chicken katsu plate from the attached S&S BBQ. The crowding, hustle and bustle of the state capital shocked him, being twice as busy as he recalled it to be. He remained determined to not let it dampen his spirits though. After finding a spot in the Ke'eaumoku Street parking garage and maneuvering through the crowds of people on foot, he was finally able to order his Hawaiian plate lunch. The chicken katsu was just as good as he remembered it to be with thin crispy strips of chicken, white rice and macaroni salad. He tried ordering the same dish back on the mainland, but it never came out as good as just about every street corner Hawaiian and Korean BBQ made it.

The jet lag caught up to him by the time he finished shopping and made his way out of Town, but the spectacular mountain view along the legendary H3 highway snapped him right out of it.

The road tunneled through the mountains in the sky, revealing epic coastal views of the island's Windward Side. He continued to drive towards Kaneohe and merged on to Route 83, continuing through Waihole Valley, with even more surreal views of the mountains and coastline. The soothing, breathtaking sights of the ocean brought him to a state of bliss. Every segment of road offered mind blowing beautiful scenery, and Orion realized he was now driving too slow, pissing off a few locals driving behind him who had seen the view a million times and just wanted to get home already. After the second lifted 'Yota with mud tires blasted by him over the double yellow lines, he picked up his pace and settled to catch up on more sight seeing the next day.

He arrived at the Mahakana North Shore beach campground just in time before the gates closed for the evening, and was further thrilled to discover the tenting site he reserved was prime.

"Now this is what I'm talking about!" he said out loud.

He walked about thirty yards down to the shore to dip his first toe in the Hawaiian ocean water again. The water was perfect and the waves were ideal for body surfing, but the sun was beginning to set and he still had to set up his tent before it got dark. He struggled a bit when attempting to pitch his rather awkward and unconventionally shaped tent, opting for it over the standard dome tent as it was twenty-two dollars cheaper, but managed to get everything set up before it was dark.

This was an experience he never had before. He hadn't known about the local camping areas during his previous visit in Oahu. Camping was strictly prohibited on Waikiki beach and most urban areas of the island due to overpopulation of tourists and homeless. Fortunately he had learned of many lesser known prime spots on the island from the friendly locals on his previous trip.

The beachfront was only a hop, skip and a jump from his camp site. He sat for a moment on the picnic table and listened to the waves as they crashed on the shore. He was happy.

The noisy chickens made their evening patrol.

"Buuuck, buck buck! Brr, Brrrr BUUUUCCCKKK!"

"I'll be waking up early in the morning anyway, let them cock-a-doodle-do all they want," Orion chuckled at them. The chickens had nearly driven him mad on his first trip to Hawaii.

He noticed there were a few others at the tent site behind him, two women and a man about his age, maybe a little older.

"Aloha, how are you guys doing?" he asked.

"Aloha!" replied the bunch simultaneously.

"Do any of you guys know where the bathrooms and showers are?"

"Why yes, as a matter of fact," the more attractive woman replied. "I was just given the tour myself. The shower is actually in that bush over there, and the bath house is that little blue cabin before the dumpsters."

"Shower in a bush?" Orion thought.

"It actually isn't bad!" the woman went on enthusiastically, reading his face. "It's pretty secluded in there too."

She motioned to a little path behind them appearing to go down a rabbit hole in the foliage. Sure enough, it led to a double spigot shower that was completely camouflaged within a cluster of huge tropical bushes.

The woman was gorgeous, with a thin complexion and long brown hair, and no makeup. She appeared to be a white girl but up close he could see she was mixed Hawaiian, and she spoke with a local accent which he found to be charming.

They struck up a conversation together again later in the evening.

He learned that her name was Nikita and she was

camping all around the island, going through some sort of personal journey as well. She had her own sharp looking Toyota Tundra with a tent attachment set up in the bed. She seemed very well equipped with her camping gear. Orion presumed she must be out here solo too, but had felt he rather not ask of any boyfriends. Apparently she hadn't known the other campers personally, and was only chatting with them when he had arrived.

The sun was now setting, and the sea breeze was picking up.

"Anyway," said Orion, "do you wanna smoke some of that pot that I got from the cab driver?"

"Yes! I'd love to. I haven't smoked in months."

"Oh good, then you won't mind that I'm a lightweight, I can probably only handle two hits."

They took more than two hits and after a few minutes they were both helplessly stoned, also forgetting how easily the sound of their conversation may have carried to the ears of the others on the beach.

"I like you," she said. "You're so funny."

"You too! I'm glad we met. I wasn't expecting to make a new friend as cool as you so quickly."

"Look at the moon," she said. "Isn't it beautiful?"

"Yes it is."

Although it wasn't quite full, it was still so bright it illuminated the campground. She started to lean closer to him as they gazed into the night sky on the tailgate of her truck. Orion began to feel butterflies in his stomach. "Surely she's into me, do I kiss her?" he thought to himself. "No way, I don't have the balls! I'll just put my arm around her."

Suddenly Nikita said, "Well, time for bed now, goodnight!"and scurried off to her tent.

Orion was perplexed. She was clearly into him, was she not? Was this an invitation to follow her to her tent? No, she zipped her tent door shut and turned off her night light. He thought over their conversation, looking for something he may have missed. She had certainly been fond of him, laughing irrationally at his bad jokes, and seeming a little nervous and goofy herself. "Maybe she just felt she was moving along too fast for someone she just met. Maybe tomorrow she'll come around tomorrow," he concluded to himself.

He dragged his feet gloomily back over to his tent only to discover that his air mattress had failed. He tried to fall asleep on the hard surface anyway. After tossing and turning for a while, he found a spot his back could tolerate and he soon drifted off into a paranoid stoned sleep.

He awoke in the middle of the night to the flashing and crashing of an unexpected thunderstorm. It was an absolute downpour. He was amazed that his tent and rainfly were holding up. Not a single drop of water made its way in. The wind and the rain was pounding the canvas so hard it sounded like a jet engine. He could hardly hear himself think. "What am I really doing out here again, so far away from home?" he wondered. Mental clarity? To rediscover a zest and inspiration for his life? To examine the job and rental markets to see if he could pull off relocating here permanently? Yes, that's it. He was only out here to test the waters and nothing more.

Right?

He slowly drifted back off to a very uncomfortable and anxious sleep.

When he awoke in the morning he felt refreshed and cast aside the worries he had overnight. He eagerly connected his devices to a wifi hotspot so he could communicate with everyone back home and get some business emails completed. Luckily he remembered to pack an AC/DC power converter for his rental car. By the time he was finished, he noticed that Nikita had already packed up all her belongings. Her tent and truck were gone!

He sighed.

He had hoped to talk to her again.

The rising sun and ocean mist was far too inviting for him to stay hung up about it. He threw on his bathing suit and walked down to the shore. The water felt chilly at first, but once he was in all the way it was perfect. In no time at all he caught a wave and body surfed it to shore. Then again, and several more. When he was finished with his swim, the campground gates had reopened for the day.

Orion jumped in his lime green Kia Soul rental that was decorated in flower decals and left the grounds in search of breakfast and coffee. Still unfamiliar with the area, as he was much further north on the island than he was during his bombed romantic getaway years prior, he quickly settled for the first McDougal's he passed. The island themed menu enhanced it a bit, with spam and rice and other fan favorites you could never get anywhere else. McDougal's was always better on the islands.

After breakfast he resumed exploring the eastern coastline of the island via 83 South. The ocean and mountain views were jaw dropping. He felt that he was already getting his money's worth out of this expedition and he was surely in the right place at the right time.

A silver Toyota highlander on mud tires passed by, and the numbers on the license plate caught his eye.

" 444"

That's odd. "444" and no other numbers on the plate. Now that he thought of it, that was the third time he had noticed those repeating numbers today. The number signs were still showing up even here, thousands of miles across the world. Something seemed off every time he had tried to attach meanings to these signs. It was difficult to distinguish if his mind was playing tricks on him or if the numbers signs were just another way of the universe attempting to communicate with him. "444" ,"747", and "222" had developed a significance to him that year that he could not explain. Even Hawaii's area code "808" had been showing up everywhere in his surroundings prior to his trip, perhaps encouraging him to go through with it.

He had researched far and wide on the significance of numerology and "angel numbers", and everyone seemed to have a different answer. He concluded which theories best resonated with his own intuition:

111: Trust your gut / New path / First instinct

222: Go for it / Don't delay / Alignment / Things are coming together at the right time

333: Things are coming together / Multiple paths crossing together / Support of the Holy Trinity

444: Protection / Have patience / Stay where you are / Trust / Keep the faith and don't give up

555: Entering 2nd phase of journey / Halfway point / Twin flame souls drawing to you / Welcome the future

666: Stop and reflect / Pause / Go back two steps / Something is in excess

777: Good fortune / Good luck is in the air / Perfect timing

888: Embrace Creativity / Infinity / Nourish your passions and creative side

999: Let go of what is unneeded / Let go of worry / Make a leap

667: Validation / New Perspective / Problem Solved / corrected

747: Don't delay / Elevate / Grow

808: Balance of money / Work / Play

If the numbers repeat in more than three digits, then the sign is more important or intense.

Later that day he managed to get in touch with one of his old friends from his previous stay on the island. Her name was Katherine, a single mom who left her hometown of Mobile, Alabama to explore the world. She found a passion for the islands where she made a living as a hospice nurse and a foreign exchange student coordinator. She had rented a room to Orion after he attempted to forge a living and stay in Hawaii after his wedding was cancelled.

He had lasted three months before coming home broke and had to start over from scratch.

He met with her back in Town and they caught up over pineapple ice cream in Waikiki.   She was apparently getting into cryptocurrency and day trading, and selling travel packages. She invited him to join her business seminar, but he hadn't the time or interest. She thought he was crazy for declining the opportunity to invest, but he was already spread thin with his own investments since he left the bio tech firm in Boston. They parted ways before sundown, and he had just enough time to get back to his campsite before the gates closed at the early 7 PM curfew. Being so close to the equator, the days typically had a 6 AM sunrise and sunset around 6:30 PM all year round.

He hopped back in his rental car, rolled a cigarette as he sheepishly read the "thank you for not smoking" sticker on the dash, and made his way back north on the Pali Highway, cruising through mountains and clouds once again.

When he was only a few miles away from the campground he noticed patches of the pavement were soaking wet. It had just rained.

"No way!" he gasped.

He had left his tent open.

Although it held up during the storm, his bedding was still damp from condensation and he figured it was a good idea to let it air dry while he was out for the day. He remembered the rain to be quite often on the Windward side but could've sworn that wasn't the case for Kahuku, the north eastern tip of the island where his camp was located.

"Shit! It was so clear and sunny this morning! After that storm last night was over with, I thought for sure it wasn't gonna come back! At least there's no way it could've rained as bad as it did last night.."

As he approached the campground the roads were soaked even worse, leaving behind deep puddles scattered everywhere. There was clearly another all out storm that had passed by while he was in Honolulu. The various ecosystems of the island never did promise consistent weather, even within a three mile radius.

He gloomily arrived at his soaking wet tent and bedding, but at least the pretty Hawaiian girl was back. She gave him a friendly "aloha" along with some snacks and drinks, but seemed to be uninterested in making further small talk or hanging out again. Certainly not interested in sharing her dry tent with him either. He laughed to himself. As soon as the sun went down she appeared to have gone to bed in her tent without making a peep.

There was a new camper in the spot between his and hers, a thin European man with glasses. Orion was unsure if he was also traveling solo. He was certainly better at camping, managing to get himself a fire going despite the ground and firewood being wet.

Orion hadn't many options at this point. He could spend a fortune on a hotel, or he could sleep in his car. But there would be too many bugs to leave the windows open. He'd have to keep the cabin sealed with the engine and A/C running all night. "Well," he said, "I suppose wasting gas is my best option at this point."

He still had a few nips of vodka in his backpack that he had purchased earlier in the day, saving them for a very moment like this one. All it took was one shot chased with an Aloha Maid and he was sound asleep in the reclined driver's seat of his car. It was only about 8:30 PM.

He awoke with a pain in his back, and tried to shift to a more comfortable position. The car was still running with plenty of gas, and the air was circulating with no exhaust fumes making their way in yet. He glanced at the clock. "What?! It's only 11 PM!"

He had hoped that most of the night had already passed. He held his hands together and prayed. "Lord, please ease my troubles tonight and help me make it to the morning. Amen."

He wasn't sure if he was really Christian or simply spiritual. He was not sure what God he prayed to, but knew something was there. It had to be. If there wasn't, then he concluded he'd prefer to stay ignorant. A preacher had shunned him before for carrying a quartz crystal and mentioning angel signs and numerology. "False doctrines," the preacher had said.

"That is not God. That is sorcery. Witchcraft." Orion didn't know what to believe. The overly religious seemed just as lost as the godless people were. He thought the belief of God choosing only one group of people to be saved was utter nonsense. How could Jesus have been God? Was he praying to Jesus, or directly to God? What was the difference? Why does it matter? Aren't all people essentially pointing to the same thing, and arguing over what name to call it?

"I don't know if I believe in Jesus, but one thing is for sure, if I go down, I'm going down with a cross in my pocket. Just in case."

On several occasions he noticed his crystals left burning sensations on his skin. Ever since he threw them out and carried a cross, he felt better. But then, what about the aliens?

"That's right!" he said, responding to his own inner dialogue. "Speaking of aliens, let's go see if there's any out there tonight!"

He turned the car off and stepped out to take a gander. The moon was so bright it illuminated the whole beach and there was hardly a need for a flash light. The wind was gnarly but felt soothing on his skin. No more rain. "If it holds up like this, all my things should be dry by the morning," he said. He continued to scan the sky for another minute.

Nothing.

No aliens.

He went back to the car to make a second attempt at falling asleep, but this time he could smell exhaust fumes mixing with the A/C as it blew into the cabin. Without the A/C running, the air got so hot and stuffy it might have been more comfortable sleeping in a wet tent. He compromised this by leaving a couple windows open just a crack, and doused his exposed skin with bug spray, hoping that would suffice. Leaving the windows open during the day was no issue, as the hot sun kept the bugs away. But at night they came out in full swing. As he drifted back to sleep, he could feel a couple fresh mosquito bites pelting his skin.

He woke up again at 3 AM, this time having to pee. He decided to take another walk around the campground and beach. He made his way to the front entrance of the grounds and discovered there were a few spots to the side of the gate that he could have parked at all along. He was warned that vehicles left parked outside of the gate were likely to get towed overnight. There were at least three other cars squeezed in this area, clearly campers that came back after curfew hours and got away with it. "Hmm... That's good to know for next time."

He was greeted by a few friendly stray cats as he made his way back to the tent. One was all black with yellow eyes, the other an orange tabby cat. They were both underweight and ragged but well adapted to the elements, and very social. The orange one meowed to Orion, begging for food. They followed him to his camp site and he gave them a few turkey slices from a lunchables he still had in his cooler. They sniffed it and scoffed, and turned back towards the gate. "Picky eaters, are ya?" Orion scolded them.

To his surprise, the sea breeze had been so intense that his tent was already dry again. The clouds parted and the stars were shining magnificently. The moon was now on the opposite side of the night sky, leaving a clear dark void of space visible overhead. He realized this was his perfect chance to stargaze. He laid back down inside the tent with a perfect view of the stars through the bug screen canopy. "I remember I used to stargaze all the time," he said. "I used to see UFO's all the time. There's gotta be something interesting happening up there.."

A few minutes went by. As beautiful as the night sky was, there were no shooting stars or UFOs.

"Have some patience, Orion. My Nana used to tell me I should be more patient. Maybe if I keep watching, I will see something."

A few moments later he noticed a faint glowing orb floating across the sky. He couldn't really see it at first, but when he looked to the side he could see it in his peripheral direction.

"There's one!" He exclaimed. Then he sighed. "Figures,

now I know those aren't aliens and that's just a satellite."

A moment after, another faint glowing orb passed by, then another one came behind it.

"Oh, wow!" he gasped. "Probably still satellites though.."

Then, to his surprise, four more glowing orbs floated across the sky one by one, and they were getting brighter.

"Must have launched half a dozen at the same time, probably *Starlink* or something," he said, still skeptical.

Then three more glowing orbs floated across the sky, this time not in single file, but in a triangle formation, the same triangle pattern as the constellation he was named after- the same triangle pattern he observed from the *"Portal of the Trees"* as he called it.

His jaw dropped. "Oh my God.. No way! There IS something out there.. Those can't be satellites! I knew it, I just knew there was something out there!"

The orbs continued to slowly pass over his head.

"Hey, where are you guys going? I'm down here!" he called out to them, hardly caring how crazy he sounded. A dimly lit cluster of distant stars began to reveal themselves behind the orbs. He gazed into them, and a feeling of weightlessness started to form in his abdomen, tickling a little. The sound of his heartbeat and the rhythm of his breath became trance-like.

"Yes! This is it! This feels so familiar..."

The cluster of stars were rapidly getting brighter. The sound of the wind and the waves crashing ashore began to fade away. A massive vibrating sensation began to surround him, and the tickle in his abdomen had intensified so greatly he thought he might explode. He was afraid, but he wanted to know what was happening so badly he could not turn away.

"Take me," he said under his breath.

Then with an exploding boom followed by a muted silence, it began.

A quantum portal opened several hundred feet over his head, and he found himself quite literally getting sucked into it.

The force of his consciousness leaving his body felt as if

he was in a rocket launch. He was exhilarated.

The sensation was unreal, like he was going through a black hole. There was no telling which way was up or down. One second he felt weightless, the next he felt like the weight of the entire Earth was crushing him.

Spinning, spinning, falling, then rising again.

The stars were gone; he could only see flashing red lights moving in a spiral direction, taking forms of sacred geometry and the fibonacci sequence.

Then as quickly as everything came, it ended with a final blinding white light.

He had arrived.

He was in a state of bliss and awe. He was unsure how much time had passed, or what time was anymore. He was simply an essence of consciousness. Then he heard a familiar deep, booming voice.

"*Greetings Traveler. We are very pleased to make your acquaintance here once again.*"

Orion's eyes shot open. He hadn't noticed they were previously closed.

He found himself sitting on a marble platform bordered by massive white pillars. The platform was nestled atop a steep hill, with hundreds upon hundreds of stone steps leading back down to the ground. There were streams of electric-blue water flowing between trees of distinct orange bark and blue-green rubbery leaves. There were purple mountains on the horizon and the sky was a scarlet-pink.

He held out his hands, and nothing was there. Then like a hologram, his hands appeared and disappeared, seeming transparent, until they came back to a solid form and remained.

"Do you recall this land, young Traveler?" the voice said again.

There was a being standing to his right. Orion turned his head but could only make out a white robe and a massive torso. When he attempted to view the figure's face, he was blinded by light. To his left side was another being, wearing a dark purple robe with a strange falcon-like head, or mask.

"I.. "I just know that I'm back where I belong," Orion finally replied.

"Indeed you are," said the being in the purple robe. "We are so proud of you. We always knew you were the chosen one." It was a woman's voice, sweet and tender, with an unusual accent, sounding like a mix of Australian and Indian.

"We have been trying to get you back here for quite some time now," replied the deep booming voice of the illuminated being. "That is, by your measure of Earthly time that is. For us, it's only been a few hours since our last encounter."

"And a most gripping few hours has it been, Traveler!" the female voice chimed in.

"Your astral magnetic field is still healing," continued the deep male voice. It took everything we had to get your attention and line you up to the portal."

"Wh.. What..??" Orion did not understand.

"Take this lad, and eat it," commanded the male voice. He held out a large blue hand with black nails. A small white fruit the size of a tangerine was in the center of his palm. Orion reached for it and ate it, without even peeling the skin first. He felt a surge of power, and he began to remember.

"*Gorhan! Katiru!* he shouted. "I had forgotten all about this place!"

It was really them. The angels of the legendary Realm 747.

The light being was Gorhan the Great, the Bridge Walker of life and death; the eternal Guide of all realms. The being with the falcon mask was the demi-goddess Katiru, the angel of fertility and courage.

"We've been observing you through the triangle," Katiru said. "You may have noticed the imprint of this multi-dimensional window showing up in your surroundings. We have always been with you."

"I knew it was you guys!" Orion exclaimed excitedly. "Err.. Well, I suppose I forgot, but only briefly of course! What was the white orange thing you guys fed me? I feel terrific!"

"It was a fruit from the tree of knowledge. It was blessed by the Lord and cleansed of evil, thus turning it white. Desperate times call for desperate measures. I was saving it for myself one day, but I felt it was better suited for you."

"Gee, thanks buddy! What a guy, huh?"

"Yes, yes, you are very welcome, however I am not so much your buddy or a guy at this moment, I'm afraid."

Orion, oblivious to Gorhan's response, continued, "boy does it feel good to be back home! Fetch me any stringed instrument, I shall play a melody for us all. Let us celebrate this reunion over some of that marvelous cosmic nectar I've been longing to taste again!"

"Your time here is brief," Gorhan insisted firmly. "Your physical body back on Earth is still heavily infected with toxins and you are not yet ready to sustain a projection like this for much longer. But now that you have consumed the fruit, your powers shall return to you at an accelerated rate, especially since you have been equipped with the quantum stones. It is still possible for you to reclaim your destiny and fulfill The Prophecy."

"I remember now... I was defeated by the System! How could I still be the chosen one? I've hardly been able to keep it together just trying to be a regular person on Earth! I don't know how I can possibly do this.."

"My son, the struggles you have endured were necessary components of your grand destiny," the deep voice of Gorhan assured him. "Your initial failure to defeat the System was also prophesied. It was necessary for you to persevere and grow stronger through the walks of conventional human life before you could be capable of wielding your true power. You are an inevitable anomaly. If you were born even one minute later or sooner, you would have missed the selective window of time."

"I don't understand.. I am only a man. How could I be the one entrusted with such a task? Surely my power could not ever compare to that of the angels. You guys could take the System out without even breaking a sweat!"

"You flatter us Traveler!" the soothing feminine voice of Katiru replied. "Alas, we are only the two hundred twenty-first and two hundred twenty-second highest commanding angels under the Archangels. The creation of the System is inevitable by all means. Every scenario where we had destroyed it in one timeline, it came back in another. Truly you are the four hundred and forty-fifth Traveler, and destined to become Moderator according to Prophecy. It is not a competition of power. It is a matter of he who was chosen to bear the key."

Orion paused, reflecting. "What is the key?"

"The key is within. When the time is right, you will know where to find it," she said.

"Wow.. Maybe I really *can* do it.. I still have a question though. What is it with the numbers? Why is it that they happen to align like that?"

"Sometimes the universe will arrange itself in patterns quite intentionally, so it may share its awareness of us, by triggering our awareness of it," Gorhan replied. "Truth be told, any attempt to further define these patterns are meaningless. These are not messages from us, although we may use them at times to get your attention. It is more so the universe simply saying "hello," or waving to you, in a sense. The universe loves its inhabitants, and is thrilled to occupy us. So much so, it will go through vast lengths just to say *"hi."* It is the one who is not God who may use logic to say, look at this pattern, clearly it means something more significant, and obsess over it. When we told Lucifer this, he did not believe. He challenged this, and obsessed over "that which makes no sense." He became suspicious of us, and left this place. He quarrelled with God, demanding the secrets of life be shared with him. *"Why would the universe go through all that effort just to say hi?"* he would say. *"Why would God create the game of life for the pleasure of it and not for a greater meaning?"* The Lord told him he already knew the answer. Yet, Lucifer chose not to believe it, since it does not make sense. He forfeited his gifts of the Holy Spirit and replaced them with pure logic. So, he came to the conclusion that *he* must be God, for him to possess the knowledge of God, and fell from grace."

"Logic has little value without wisdom," Katiru added. "The one who is of God understands and knows that logic is to be used only as a tool, not the foundation, lest they lose their minds, or hearts, or both. For everlasting life in Christ is insatiable to logic, yet it is the truth."

"Everlasting life in Christ..? Oh wow, so he's really real? Is he like, the boss of everything?"

"Indeed He is. He has revealed Himself as other characters too, to various cultures and populations throughout time, but as for us and our house, we shall serve the Lord," Katiru answered.

What do the archangels do then? Is this not heaven? I thought *this* was the highest point in the universe," Orion said, baffled.

"This *is* the highest point in the universe and this *is* heaven," Gorhan replied. "Heaven was created as a gift, a place to seek all of our lives to find- a destination to move towards in all that we do. It is here, at the highest realm in the universe, that one is closest to the Kingdom and thus our Creator. Here, there is no pain, there is only amazement, vigor and joy. Down yonder into the valley lies the gate, where all timelines intersect at one single point and all ancestors and relatives may rejoice and visit each other from all realms. The universe is a container for creation, but is not all that is."

"Wow, that's right. It's all coming back to me now," Orion said.

"We the angels, and some two hundred others are the supervisors of heaven and Earth. The Archangels guard the Kingdom. They are not bound to creation like we are. They may enter and exit the universe at any time."

"The Kingdom?" Orion inquired. I thought God was in heaven and the Kingdom was the same thing."

"Nonsense Traveler," Gorhan replied. "Don't you remember? The Lord is the holder of our universe. It is by the tip of His very finger that the cosmos are held in place...."

Gorhans' voice trailed off into an echo. Suddenly Orion's surroundings flashed white, and he could see nothing. He felt a sensation of free falling. Then he could feel and hear the wind whipping all around him.

He opened his eyes.

He was already back in his tent on the beach.

The sun was shining and the birds were chirping.

"What- what happened?" he said, mesmerized. He tried frantically to recollect his memory. He could remember star gazing, and seeing the UFOs- and then feeling an intense pressure encompass him followed by a loud boom.

Surely he had just fallen asleep, hadn't he?

He could vaguely remember dreaming of a white palace-like structure with marble pillars. Then a voice.. Voices? There was a feeling like he had reunited with a long lost relative, but couldn't put his finger on it. All he knew is that something special had happened, and he was closer to whatever he came out here to find.

Orion stepped out of his tent and took a deep breath of the fresh island air. He threw on his bathing suit and jumped in the waves for a refreshing morning swim. Then he gathered his belongings and went to search for his first meal of the day.

Orion resumed his vacation as usual, driving around the island, trying new foods from various vendors and visiting his favorite beaches. But there was another thing he intended to check off his to-do list. He had brought his electric guitar with him in his checked baggage. For years he had dreamed of playing his electric guitar in Hawaii. He hadn't brought it on his previous trip and regretted it. His amp was too heavy to bring on the plane so he found a cheap DJ speaker for sale locally, and set his course for Sandy's, the lesser known big wave beach on the south shore.

When he got to Sandy's he found a prime parking spot in the front row, close to the only shaded area that was nestled beside the beach showers and bathrooms. He set up his camp chair with his guitar and portable speaker. The battery was fully charged and the strings were in tune.

Drat!

His sound effect pedal wasn't working. Perhaps he should have just brought an acoustic guitar.

He went back to his car and smoked the roach he still had from his first night with Nikita. Now feeling enhanced with the help of some tropical marijuana, he excitedly returned to his makeshift stage by the bathrooms and began to play anyway. The DJ speaker allowed him to plug in his guitar and play over background music on a separate channel, so he creatively put on some local island jams and layered his own improvised guitar riffs on top of them. Despite the absence of distortion or echo without his effects pedal, he managed to dish out some groovy reggae style tunes and one of the locals complimented him as he passed by. Then after about an hour, he felt it was time to take a swim break.

The lifeguards made announcements on megaphones every ten minutes for everyone to get out of the water. "There is no need for anyone to be swimming in the water right now! Please step away from the shoreline. Mahalo."

Nonetheless a dedicated group of surfers and swimmers stayed in the water. Bobbing up and down over the waves, some riding them to shore, others wiping out big time. The waves were not as big as the west coast pipeline, but big enough, and today's surf was up to ten feet, even bigger than usual. What made this beach dangerous was the sudden drop off as the waves crashed on shore, instead of a smooth and gradual landing. This increased the strength of the current and riptide, and even just six inches of water at the shoreline carried enough force to grab one's feet and drag them in.

Orion examined the waves. He was a very skilled swimmer, and was determined to go in. He dared to approach the water. He was not even knee deep before the splash and crash of each wave fought to suck him under. It took all of his strength to remain planted in the sand. He was thrilled, and feeling more confident. He figured that the most dangerous part was where he was standing, and he should swim out far enough to float over the waves before they crashed on shore. That was what the experienced swimmers appeared to be doing. The group of local surfers made it seem near effortless to stay afloat over the passing waves.

He took in a deep breath of air and continued full force into the water. He jumped over a few smaller waves, which still had enough force to knock him down if he missed, and swam out just far enough to try body surfing the first bigger wave. He managed to catch it, and it launched him back to shore, nearly tearing off his bathing suit. Before he could stand, another wave from behind crashed into him and knocked him down. It took everything he had to crawl back to the shore before getting sucked right back in. He caught his breath, drank some water and then hurried back, this time diving under the waves and rushing past the cut off point where they crashed down, eventually making his way out far enough to simply stay floating over them before they began to part.

But something was wrong.

The current was still sucking him out further.

Now he was well past the local guys.

He realized those guys had diving flippers. This was a dangerous move he had made without even a boogie board. He remembered his swim lessons as a boy at summer camp. He had even passed the lifeguard test in high school and worked briefly at the city pool. He flipped on his back and started using the elementary backstroke. It appeared to generate enough momentum to change his direction back to the shore. He swam ferociously. One of the other guys noticed Orion was struggling, and approached him with their board.

"Hey braddah, you need help?" the young Hawaiian swimmer asked.

"No thanks, I'm good. I used to be a lifeguard," replied Orion.

The local nodded and continued on his way, searching for a wave to catch.

A few moments later Orion had made enough distance back to shore to break free from the current, but the waves were now crashing over him, hardly allowing him to resurface quick enough to catch his breath.

"Oh my God," he thought. "I can't breathe. Is this really how I'm going to go out?"

Exhausted and panting, he just barely made it to shore without drowning, and he felt foolish. He suspected the others had watched him. With his ego bruised he tried to play it off like nothing, and walked up to the showers to rinse the sand from his pockets, hair and ears. He reassured himself it was still worth it, as the waves were incredibly exciting, and he had fun, besides the moment at the end that is. Perhaps if he trained hard enough he could swim those waves like nothing some day. Maybe even learn to surf the mega pipeline waves on the West side.

He was amazed by the fitness and talent of the surfers. He longed to be like them.

There were so many beautiful wāhine on the beach it was mindblowing. How incredible would it be to land one of these babes and fall in love again, he thought. But he wasn't here for romance this time. There was something else he was searching for, something important.

Or was it?

Was he really on the verge of a major breakthrough or did he just simply need a vacation?

It was his final night of camping before relocating to a room in Kaneohe in the morning.

It was time for a real bed and shower.

He left the rain-fly off his tent hoping to view the stars again, but it was too cloudy. As he was drifting off to sleep, he felt a raindrop on his nose. He instantly woke up, jumped out of the tent and secured the rain-fly.

He wasn't going to let a repeat of his second night happen again.

In the morning he packed up his camp and took a final dip in the ocean. The waves were docile compared to Sandy's, but still bigger than they ever got at the beaches he was used to back home. He took some final pictures, hopped in his rental car and hit the road.

Something had him feeling off and he couldn't seem to shake it. Kelsey had flown out with him on his first trip to Oahu. She was very beautiful, perhaps even more than Sadie, but lived a dangerous and dramatic lifestyle, struggling with alcohol dependency and prescription meds. He had hoped a radical change in her environment would bring out her better side. For a time it did, until she broke into the condo owner's wine cellar and got them both thrown out. She had an opportunity to stay on the islands with Orion after he had secured the room from Katherine, but she refused the job he had lined up for her and flew back to Boston.

The memories of her love and deception clashed within his mind.

When he reached his room he began to feel better. It was the spare bedroom in the same condo overlooking Kaneohe Bay, the same as he stayed at before. The property owner sympathized with Orion after learning the truth about Kelsey and permitted him to come back granted he would occupy the room alone.

He flopped down on the bed. It was so nice to lie down in a real bed again. The breeze coming in through the screen door was most pleasant. Air conditioning was seldom needed. The weather was always perfect.

After he was settled, he headed out to the Windward Mall to find something to eat, and got a lau-lau plate with some fresh pineapple juice. By the time he had returned it was only 6:30 PM, yet he was exhausted.

He finished unpacking his suitcase and laid back down on

the queen size bed. He quickly drifted off to sleep. He tossed and turned through the night, waking several times despite feeling relaxed and at ease.

Before he knew it, the early rays of the sunrise had begun peeking through his window. Not ready to wake up, he covered his eyes with a blanket and fell back asleep, and dreamt of a naked woman wrapped in a white bed sheet on the beach, motioning for him to come towards her.

His eyes shot open and he awoke instantly without blinking.

"That's it," he said. "I'm going to Halo beach."

Halo beach was on the northwest tip of the island, and was known to accommodate women swimming completely in the nude. Despite losing the cut of his muscles over the years he decided now wasn't the time to be insecure. Perhaps he was destined for some romance on this trip. Perhaps a group of topless women would welcome him at the beach.

He was still a man.

He changed his outfit, brought a bed sheet and some nips of vodka in a beach bag and set sail for the H2 highway.

When arrived, he saw more cars in the parking lot than he had expected. "Probably just a ton of dudes here," he thought. He felt a little silly for thinking he might come across naked women on the beach that would invite him to sunbathe with him, a total stranger.

But he had already come this far.

When he made his way up the path to the beach entrance immediately there were two naked women lying in the shade under a tree. They were native, with cacao brown skin, beautiful and thick. They appeared to be a couple however, and he had a gut feeling not to disturb them.

He walked further down to the left side of the beach. He could have sworn he did see a lone woman in the distance- perhaps she was the one from his dream. As he made his way over, he discovered there was indeed a beautiful woman isolated on the far left side of the beach, but she was clothed and had a small child with her. He figured she best not be disturbed either.

He noticed the water was much lower than he remembered it to be the last time he was there with Kelsey. Although the beach was just as beautiful, the low tide revealed many sharp and jagged rocks and hardly seemed ideal for swimming.

He looped around on the trail back to the other side of the beach past the fisherman, the area of the beach where those who desired to tan without tan lines were more likely to be found.

Orion had only made several steps on the other side of the beach and almost immediately there she was: An absolutely beautiful mixed race island girl, completely in the nude, running to the shoreline for a swim. She was decorated in tattoos, with a perfect hourglass figure, gauged ear piercings and a defined exotic face with a bright white smile. Orion approached her trying not to seem too obvious. He stripped down to his underwear and swam next to her. She cast him a quick shy smile and returned back to the beach and began dressing.

Orion stayed in the water a moment, then walked back up to the sand, pleased to discover she had settled right next to where he had placed his belongings down.

"Okay, think Orion.. What do I even say to her?" He recalled the beach bag. He had brought a few shots of vodka but forgot the cans of iced tea for a chaser. He tried to think of a smooth pick up line.

He semi-confidently approached her and said, "hi there, how are you?"

She smiled. "I'm well thanks, how are you?"

Her smile reassured him a bit.

"I'm great! Would you like a shot?" Orion held out the little nip of vodka.

"Oh, no thank you," she replied. "I don't drink."

"Oh well, that's ok," he said. "Well I must say then, the only thing more beautiful than this ocean, is this ocean, with you in it."

She did not seem to favor him.

"Thank you, but I must get back to reading my book now," she said.

"Oh, no," he thought frantically. "I thought that was a pretty good one.. Damn! Why are women so complicated? Maybe I'm just not hot right now.. I need a shredded bod again! I used to have the babes all over me when I'd go to the beach!"

Then something caught him by surprise. Amongst the mystery woman's tattoos, he noticed there was "222" printed on her finger.

"Oh!" he exclaimed instantly. "Is that "222" tattooed on your finger? That's an angel number! I see that number everywhere and I still can't quite get its meaning down."

She smiled and replied, "it means alignment."

Orion was at a loss for words and stumbled back to his bed sheet on the sand and pondered.

"222 means alignment.. It seems everyone has an entirely different meaning for these repeating numbers," he thought. "What the hell does this really mean?"

He sat and thought deeper. There was definitely something significant about this woman and the sign of her tattoo. Did this mean she actually *was* destined to make his acquaintance and he should try to stir up conversation again? But she was clearly more interested in her book and gave him the signal that she would rather be left alone. Orion felt something screaming within his intuition.

"*222 means alignment*, she said. Am I out of alignment? I came out here to re-align and balance myself, how could I still be out of alignment?"

Then it hit him like a freight train.

"*We are the two hundred twenty-first and two hundred twenty-second commanding angels under God*" echoed in his subconscious.

All at once, he remembered everything. The 747th realm. Gorhan and Katiru. The System. Jostania. His mission; his destiny.

He quickly packed up his belongings and rushed back to

his car. He had to write down everything before he forgot again. He searched Joogle Maps for the nearest library. He found one in a local town a few miles away that he had never been to before.

It was a rather intimidating place. The outside seemed run down and like a hotspot for theft. But as he made his way inside, he was relieved to see the library had an inviting vibe. It was very clean and well kept. The woman at the front desk greeted him kindly.

"Aloha, how may I help you?" she asked.

"Aloha," Orion replied. "Could I please use a computer?"

"Yes, I can print you a guest pass for one hour."

He quickly signed in to his cloud storage and wrote down everything he could remember.

Orion, you are the chosen one. You are the 445th Traveler and the prophecy is real. The dreams were real. The System is real. You are the only one who can stop it. You have the ability to bend time and manipulate reality.

Orion stared at the screen, drawing a blank.

"How did I used to do it though?" he thought. "How? Think, think..."

He focused on the digital clock on the computer screen.

"Think.. Reverse the clock.. Manipulate time.."

But no matter how hard he tried, nothing changed.

Then he heard Katiru's voice speak to him.

"With stress, fear or doubt, one can not surpass the third dimension and its laws. The only way to remove these limitations is to remove the belief they were ever there to begin with.

"That's right," he said. "I'm trying too hard. I'm feeling stressed and doubtful. I have to simply believe, without any strain or stress, and it will happen."

The clock read 3:32 PM. Orion declared under his breath, "it is 3:31 PM."

The digits on the clock immediately went back one, and read 3:31PM.

It didn't startle or shock him. Instead it brought him great relief. It was like breaking out the old baseball glove, loosening up the fibers again and finally making that perfect catch.

He could feel the deep vibrations returning and his consciousness beginning to exit the physical realm. He closed his eyes. He floated back a few feet from his body, still watching the clock on the computer screen. Then he snapped his fingers. All at once the numbers on the clock began to violently change. Shadows of people entering and exiting the library appeared, then disappeared, moving in fast forward motion. The sun started going up and down, day turning to night and then back to day in just seconds. Orion's body stayed seated where he was, and no one seemed to notice him.

He snapped his fingers again and whispered, *"return to the present."*

Immediately the clocks stopped at 3:33 PM. He tethered back to his body and it was like nothing happened.

Everyone else in the library was still focused on their own studies, carrying on with the same conversations. "I can't believe it," he thought. "Dr. Switch and the time crystal stone thingies were real! I will not let his death be in vain."

Orion closed his computer session and exited the library. Suddenly he felt nauseous and very weak, and like he was about to lose control of his bowels. He hurdled over in pain. He realized his body wasn't yet strong enough to expend this kind of energy again. He breathed slowly and concentrated on re-aligning his chakras until he felt well enough to drive.

He headed back to the Windward side in a daze. The beauty of the mountains and scenery weren't as compelling to him now. He was still in shock from regaining his memories and abilities. Fortunately when he got back to the condo the other tenants weren't there. He could be alone.

He sat down in a big white chair next to the screened patio and began to think. "Damn it. My body can't even handle this power anymore."

He glanced at the clock. It was 4:30 PM. No time to waste. Another session of big waves at Sandy beach would be the perfect way to get in a work out. He had to start strengthening his physical body, and fast. He was still feeling slightly ill but knew once he got himself back in the water he would feel better.

When he got to the beach the crowding was much greater than it was during his previous visit that week. "Must be 'cause it's the weekend now," he said. He hadn't realized how lucky he was to have snagged the parking spot up front by the bathrooms last time. He had to drive the length of a few football fields down past the prime swimming area before he was able to find a spot. "Should I just take another lap around and find someone that might be on their way out?" he looked around. The sky was a rich cobalt blue and the mountains were vividly green. "Nah, I should enjoy the walk. It's beautiful out."

He approached the edge of the beach, still about a hundred yards away from the prime spot with big waves and smooth sand. He had totally forgotten about the women and his male biology until within moments of stepping foot on the beach he was already surrounded by girls.

"How'd ya like da cheeks today, braddah?" he overheard some surfers chatting. "Stellar, brah!" the other replied.

Orion laughed out loud.

Stellar was an understatement. There were women stretching and relaxing, some alone, others in groups, and to make matters even more baffling, there were hardly any men. There were ladies upon ladies as he walked the start of the beach, and with the most revealing bathing suits, displaying their bodies for all to see in the hot Hawaiian sun.

He felt a lump form in his throat.

Orion made it to the prime spot and placed his belongings by a downed log and some shrubs. He sloppily applied sunscreen, then realized he forgot his bathing suit, so he left on his jean shorts and made a run for the water anyway.

This time he had no fear of drowning. He swam effortlessly over and under the waves. It was exhilarating whilst it was therapeutic, the excitement masking the vigorous workout of it all. As soon as he felt fatigued, he swam back to the shore, underestimating the strength of the current again, and nearly collapsed with exhaustion in the sand.

He made his back to his spot by the logs and bushes. Two European models had come and laid down their belongings and towels next to his while he was out swimming, but they were already on the other part of the beach posing and taking pictures of each other. He scanned the view. More girls, surfers, and lifeguards. A few families were setting up tables with plates of food. The sun was setting. It was time to call it a day.

He went to bed swiftly that night, feeling rather satisfied and complete with his day. He hadn't dared to attempt summoning his powers again. His body needed more time to strengthen.

He awoke at 3AM after a series of troubling dreams.

Sadie had been sitting beside him on his bed.

His first love.

Her mother was sitting across from them in a doctor's waiting room chair. It would appear that his room had turned into a delivery room.

And Sadie had just given birth.

Sadie and her mother, Melissa, had been chatting. Melissa turned her attention to Orion.

"Yes indeed," she said, nodding. "It *is* a good thing he made these changes with his life. It brings a mother such joy to know her daughter is in the hands of a good husband."

Sadie smiled eagerly. "That's right mom! He has really done it. He's truly a changed man. We're getting married in the morning."

A nurse came into the NICU with an infant in a cradle on wheels.

"She is five weeks early, but she is already breathing unassisted. Would you like to hold your daughter, Orion?" the nurse said. She was a slightly portly middle aged woman with circle frame glasses and an ear to ear smile.

Orion was at a loss for words.

The nurse carefully scooped up the baby bundled in a blanket and gently placed her in Orion's arms.

Instantly Orion felt a warm sensation in his belly as soon as the child made contact with him.

He held her awkwardly, his arm and wrists cramping a bit, as she seemed so comfortable just as she as he'd rather not dare to reposition himself.

All of the pain in his heart and soul instantly lifted.

The love of the baby completely filled the void in his soul and all of his suffering dissipated.

Then two men dressed like FBI agents with tuxedos, black sun glasses, and wireless headsets burst through the door.

"She isn't yours," one of the men said, as he came over and removed the baby from Orion's arms.

Sadie and her mother disappeared.

Everything turned black.

He opened his eyes again.

He was lying on the ground.

It was cold, damp and clammy.

The sun was peeking through the foliage, it appeared to be a crisp spring morning.

As he stood up, he saw that he was in front of his old lake house, the one in Linensburg before his parents divorced.

There was a circle gravel driveway and a red Ford Escort parked in the center.

A child was left alone strapped to a booster seat in the back of the car, crying, screaming.

Orion, hearing the child's cries, rushed over to the car.

The child was still a baby, no more than two years of age.

He was precious.

He hadn't grown any hair yet, only a soft peach fuzzed head. He had chubby cheeks and hands. He was wearing a mini dress suit with suspenders and a bow tie.

The child made eye contact with Orion, but his presence appeared to give him no comfort or reassurement. The child looked away from him and continued sobbing.

Orion desperately tried to open the door but it was jammed.

The child continued to weep, terrified and abandoned.

Orion saw the child was in pain. It was then, all other aspects of reality left his mind. His only purpose and reason to be alive at this moment was to rescue the child.

He frantically punched the window. Over and over again. It would not break.

He caught his breath and thought for a moment. If he broke the glass it could land on the baby! How could he have been so foolish? He should try the front driver's side window instead.

He punched the glass with all of his might and it shattered on the first blow, his knuckles oozing with blood.

He realized the front door had been unlocked.

He rushed in the car and reached to the back seat for the baby. He picked him up and sat with him on the ground outside of the car, holding him tightly to his chest.

He gazed into the baby's eyes.

It was then he realized the baby was himself, the spitting image of the child in a photograph that hung up in his family's living room.

They both sobbed and clung to each other.

"I'm so sorry," Orion said. "It's ok now. Nothing is going to hurt you. See? I'm here. Nothing can get you buddy. There will be nothing bad now that I'm here."

The child eased his sobs, and started sucking his thumb. Orion rocked him back and forth, and within moments he was asleep.

The warm feeling returned in his belly, and the void in his heart was gone.

"I will be your shield, child," Orion whispered to him. "Nothing will ever harm you. You will always be safe in my arms."

It was shortly after that he awoke, and realized it was all a dream.

◆ ◆ ◆

Ring. Ring. Ring.

"Sorry I missed your call! Please leave a message after the beep."

"Hey Mom, it's me. I'm just calling to let you know I'm coming home early. Ok, talk to you later. Love you, bye."

Orion was deeply emotionally disturbed since his dream of being separated from the child, and then witnessing himself as a child weeping in the back seat of a car, abandoned- only to awake and discover that both children were gone.

It hadn't helped much that he had never stopped loving Sadie. They had briefly gotten back together after high school, but her new boyfriend had him outmatched at the time, and she went back to him and got pregnant. Orion insisted the baby was his, but DNA proved otherwise.

He had suppressed his grief and forgotten about it, until now. Since Sadie's daughter was born, she had married, divorced, and even had a few more kids. He had managed to get in touch with her again in his late 20's, but he cancelled his date with her to run back to Kelsey. Sadie deeply regretted giving him another chance, and refused to speak to him ever again.

Orion had to keep moving to escape the grief.

The busier he stayed, the easier it was to forget about it. He had to make sure no one knew how devastated he was. His family and friends were expecting him to come back home happy and tan.

He went down to Waikiki to get some souvenirs to bring home. First stop was the Don Quijote superstore. They had everything. Food, booze, knick knacks, even vintage video games and comics. Various food vendors and shops branched off of the superstore. This part of town was a little rough but the market was still the best, with deals that couldn't be found anywhere else on the island.

As soon as he walked in he found the section of the store dedicated to souvenirs and coffee. He got a great selection of gifts to return home with, including a tiki bottle opener for his dad and shaka braddah playing guitar for his own little present. He decided to pass on the greasy food vendors outside, as he hadn't been feeling so well.

He left the store and navigated over to the Diamond Head side of Waikiki and found an oceanfront restaurant. They had a bar on the second floor with seats overlooking the ocean.

Perfect.

He ordered an overpriced cheeseburger and pink mixed drink, just to check it off his list.

He observed the crowds of people excitedly hustling and bustling to and fro the beach below him. "Yep, this is paradise alright," he lied to himself.

No amount of money or tropical vacations could fill the void in his heart.

The next morning he finished packing up and headed to the airport.

The trip was over.

CH. 6

The Big Bang

He woke up to the sound of his phone ringing. He rolled over in his bed, searching for it on the lamp desk, his eyes still closed.

"Hello?"

"Orion, I'm so sorry I haven't spoken to you in so long."
It was Sadie.

"..Sadie..? What a nice surprise to hear your voice again. Don't feel bad. You didn't know what else to do. I'm so sorry for-"

"Stop right there," she interrupted. "There's no need for you to apologize to me anymore. Your mistakes are nothing but whispers in the wind now. You changed who you are as a person and already tried giving the world to me. It was my mistake to miss out on that by holding a grudge."

"Well you wouldn't have had to hold a grudge if I didn't ruin everything in the first place."

"No, I ruined everything.. If I hadn't cheated on you when we were kids-"

"It doesn't matter anymore. I still love you Sadie."

"I– I still love you too."

"Sadie, have you ever had dreams of us over the years? Dreams where you and I were holding each other again?

"Yes."

"Did you get that same warm fuzzy feeling in your belly, even though it was completely imaginary?"

No response.

"Sadie? Are you still there? Sadie!"

The line suddenly went dead. White foam began spewing from the phone, melting the plastic with a terrible hiss.

Then the entire room began to melt.

Orion screamed in terror.

Then he woke up instantly in his bed, this time for real.

It was only a dream.

The pain in his heart was too great to bear.

He jumped out of bed and ran out the door. He ran, ran, and ran. He ran in bare feet. He ran with no shirt on. He ran without even going to the bathroom first. He ran until the pain in his feet forced him to go back home to restart his day correctly, and then he left the house running again, with no set course or direction.

He would only stop at gas stations or supermarkets he passed by to get enough food and water to fill him for several hours until he needed to stop again. When the pain in his legs and feet became too great, he would walk. When he could no longer walk, he did pushups.

He did this for the next two months without a single care about any bills, health insurance, a car; nothing. His residual income provided him with enough money for food, water and vitamins and that's all he did. He did not communicate with his parents or family anymore. He didn't care what they thought. All he cared about was escaping the pain. The pain in his body from the persistent exercise was the only thing that could dull the pain in his mind and heart.

By the time the sun went down he would turn back for home, oftentimes not getting back until well after midnight. He would fall fast asleep from the exhaustion, and repeat the same cycle in the morning all over again when he woke up.

He no longer desired to smoke or drink. He no longer

desired to make money or meet women.

He had another plan.

By the third month of his doing this, he had completely transcended his pain and was hardly still aware of his physical body as he ran. He began to astral project so vividly every night that the line between real and unreal began to disappear.

Then it happened.

On the seventeenth day of the third month of his thirty-first year, Orion finally managed to astral project to the place of his first vision: The windmill.

This time when he was met by the great white light at the end of the tunnel, he did not have fear.

He dove right into it.

By the time the Traveler realized what he had done, it was too late.

He had left the universe.

He could see the entire circle of life and time as we know it.

There was no beginning or end.

It was a loop.

The Big Bang had marked the end whilst simultaneously creating the beginning of the universe; the result of two opposing forces expanding within a container until the container popped.

The universe, however, was not all of existence in totality.

It would appear that our universe was only one of many within a continuous, rotating, everlasting wheel of many universes, endlessly stacked upon each other, each one being like a single page in a book that was a mile thick.

It was then, he realized his life on Earth and the universe we resided in, was small.

For a brief moment, he was in a state of bliss.

However, something was wrong.

He couldn't stop.

He continued to exit the universe, losing all control of his life along with it. The things he had taken for granted in being alive- gravity firmly planting him to the ground, the involuntary beating of his heart and the breathing of his lungs; his memories, his identity- all began to slip away from his grasp. There was nothing he could do except hold on in terror, desperate to avoid the doom of what he initiated: His death.

For in lifting the curtain of reality and exposing the grand picture, he had also exposed the Creator; and unauthorized was he to do such a thing!

And now he could not undo it.

He could not stop it from taking place.

It was too late to turn back.

The ethereal cord that suspended his consciousness continued to stretch, further and further out of the cosmos. He held on with all of his might. He felt like he was dangling off of a cliff, his fingers only moments from giving out.

He could see that out of the entire contents of the omniverse, it was only our universe that was being paid attention to; being held in place by something.

The Creator.

All of the other universes were lifeless.

Out of the uncountable others He could have chosen, it was only ours the Creator was pouring life unto.

Mankind won the lottery on a grand scale.

And mankind had forgotten.

The Traveler previously thought the Creator would appear differently than this.

A belief he felt most foolish for thinking now.

For it had already been written, "*God created mankind in His own image.*"

However, God was not a man, per se.

He was a Child.

The Perfect Child.

To the right hand side of the Child was His Mother in illuminating light.

The Perfect Mother.

In scale to these beings, the Traveler was only a tiny spec, perhaps lesser than that.

The universe in scale to the Creator was no larger than His hand.

The omniverse contained our universe, which our universe was only a small segment of. Each universe, or segment, appeared to be the same size, or close to it. No universe spanned wider than His hand, but the total length of the omniverse extended into infinity like a neverending rope.

The Child was seated within something, but it was not a King's chair of solid gold. It appeared like a round activity center, like that of which a human baby may enjoy sitting in–but more advanced.

It was then, he realized this was the Throne.

Instead of dolls or baby rattles, the planets and the constellations were laid before it like toys; ornaments.

How these were observable as separate from the universe was an enigma. Perhaps it was a cosmic window the Creator used to zoom in and out of the universe.

It was then, he realized the Perfect Child was the Holy Ghost of Christ Jesus.

It was then, he realized the Perfect Mother was Mary, the Virgin Mother of God.

The Lord held the universe in place above His head by a series of ethereal cords attached to the tip of His finger, halting the rotation of the omniverse.

God was very, very, very big.

It was then, the Traveler remembered the key: His inner child.

For it is only as a child that man is sinless, and in a familiar image to the Creator.

The Creator does not recognize Himself in men that have abandoned their inner child. For these men, there is no longer anything to distinguish them any differently from the beasts of the land that slaughter each other for mating rights and consume each other out of survival instinct.

As Orion realized he was dying, he cared little that his

possessions on Earth would turn to dust, or how his works would become forgotten and meaningless. All he could think about was how hurt his mother would be at his loss. The love in his heart was the only thing that gave him the strength to continue clinging to his life.

There was no pain he would not bear to protect the child that used to be him and his mother from the grief of his absence. The worst grief. The ultimate grief. The grief that Mary experienced; the highest pain in the universe- a mother losing her son.

Mary reached out Her hand and brought Orion up to Her. She scolded him.

He became like a child, apologized and begged for mercy.

He looked to Jesus.

He could only see the side of His face.

He appeared to be no more than four or five years old.

Orion recognized himself in Him, but he was not Him. Yet, he loved Him. The Holy Ghost of Christ reminded him of the brother, or perhaps the younger son he never had.

The Holy Ghost was the embodiment of the highest mind of the universe.

All consciousness stemmed from Him.

Time passed by differently here. Orion now understood that the entire duration of his life on Earth was extremely brief, the equivalent of only thirty-five minutes or so in this dimension. Time only appeared to go much slower for humans because they were scaled down, and very, very, very small.

With this discovery came a deep melancholy and shame.

He realized that his life was essentially meaningless, and the Creator was trying to protect him from this truth- but Orion had barged right in to the projector room of the theater, completely disregarding the "Do Not Enter" sign so to speak, demanding more knowledge and power in his selfish pursuit of pleasure.

Now he knew.

Now he knew there was no greater purpose of life, at least

not to man.

The Creator held the universe and loved it so, like a child cherishes a worn teddy bear and refuses to exchange it for a new one.

Nothing that took place on Earth mattered. It was all for the glory of God- a game simply played for the joy of the Child-like Creator and nothing more.

It turned out we humans may just be the characters within the mind of Christ, merely instruments of His grand orchestra.

Orion had exposed this.

However, he didn't care.

Since nothing really mattered, and nothing was real, everything might as well still matter and be real then.

If he died, he would break his mother's heart; he would break his inner child's heart.

So he refused to let go of his life lest he harm his mother or child.

Mary gazed into Orion's eyes.

Her look of scorn quickly softened and she smiled at him.

Truly She was the epitome of grace.

He woke up in a daze. He had been lying in a damp patch of sand for an unknown period of time. He tried to make out his surroundings but his vision was still blurry. He stood up, brushed off his jeans, and slowly his eyes adjusted to the light again. It appeared to be a late summer day. The sun permeated the edges of the horizon yet several grey clouds were staining the sky with darkness. There was a peculiar building in the distance about fifty yards from where he stood.

So he went to it.

It appeared to be a heavily aged, two story tall schoolhouse of dark rotting brick with a stained concrete foundation. Beside it was a small playground partially shaded by a few sickly looking, semi-dead trees. It was a schoolyard, and an eerie one at that. The ground was mostly bare with a few straggly patches of crabgrass. Then, he heard faint chattering in the wind.

He realized he wasn't alone.

Suddenly there were children of various ethnicities at play. They were laughing as they ran around chasing each other, appearing to be giddy and worry free. They didn't seem to notice him. A pang of anxiety penetrated his core. Something was off.

The air was unusually thick and unpleasantly raw within his nostrils. An unsettling odor revealed itself. It smelled like blood and rotting flesh, with a hint of gasoline. He could have sworn he set his course for The Land of Flowing Waters, as he called it. How did he end up here? This was not the spectacular world he was supposed to return to.

"It can't be.." he murmured.

It was as if he was awake in the real world, or as he simply called it, the Real. He could sense his physical limitations and the harsh weight of gravity on his body. This was odd, since typically when he was in his astral form, his senses felt pleasantly enhanced. His body would feel light as a feather. He would see more vividly, hear with more clarity, and his feelings, especially that of love, would attach more deeply to the root of his soul. The worries of everyday life would slip his mind. There would be a warm buzzing sensation from within. His earthly identity and age would disappear.

Yet, there he stood in this strange schoolyard sticking out like a sore thumb. His memory of the previous events had not yet returned. All he knew was that he was far away from home. A chilly breeze passed through his white t-shirt giving him goosebumps. The sky was a strange orange hue yet there was no sight of the sun. He tried to wake up but he couldn't. He was fully conscious. This was real.

The children continued to frolic and play in the playground. A little brown skinned girl with dark frizzy hair, blue overalls and a yellow t-shirt appeared to be moving in slow motion as she spun the roundabout with a big grin on her face. She had lost her bottom baby teeth, and small pearl white knobs protruded upwards from her gums in their place. Her giggles echoed, failing to sync with the movements of her mouth. It was as if time was glitching.

Suddenly he could feel a massive vibration begin to surround him and radiate through his chest. He glanced up and froze in terror. Approaching overhead was a massive black aircraft, resembling the shape of a flattened blimp, with an endless array of equipment dangling from the shell like mechanical vines. Tiny green specks of light emitted from various places, with a red glowing orb of energy propelling the craft in its rear center.

"Are they here for me?" he stammered. "What's happening!?"

He quickly ran to the children and shouted for them to run inside the school, but they were in a trance. They seemed unaware of the coming danger, and could not hear him. They did not make eye contact with him. Then, like a flame flickering in and out, the image of the children disappeared.

It was a hologram.

The last of the living children that attended the school had been dead for years. This was a trap that had been set for him.

He dashed for the schoolhouse and burst through the front double doors. He collapsed on the first flight of stairs, paralyzed with fear. He peeked out of the stairwell window, trying to stay out of view. He closed his eyes.

"Definitely just a bad dream," he pleaded to himself. "I can make everything go away. This is all in my head. Maybe if I just keep trying to go back to sleep, I'll eventually wake up safely in my bed."

Alas, there was no escape. He remained there, a sitting duck.

A high pitched whining sound like that of a dentist's drill was approaching. He glanced out of the stairwell window.

It was here.

A tall, slender, extraterrestrial figure arrived at the schoolyard. It glided effortlessly through the air without the use of any visible propellers or fans. The System was now so advanced, the drone bots had evolved into living, breathing, human-like machines. In place of bones it had a skeleton of titanium rods and shafts, lacking the presence of flesh or clothing to mask its ghastly appearance, paired with a hideous, bulbous, elongated cranium with dim green lights for eyes. Its hands and fingers were composed of sharp, needle-like rods that could interchange into a variety of different tools and weapons like a Swiss army knife.

A deep pit of doom sunk down his throat. He remembered now. He thought he had more time before something like this could happen. He was caught completely off guard and was unprepared.

"Please forgive me Lord," he prayed under his breath. "I didn't know what I was getting myself into. It was an accident. Please spare me. Holy Mary, mother of God, thank you for your Son Jesus. Please let Him stay with me if only a little longer… Please don't let the story end so soon."

What was supposed to be another leisurely stroll through the cosmos turned out to be a horrific accident, as he was intercepted in crossing back to Earth via the Astral Gate, and sent to the future reality of his own world instead. His attempt to hide was futile. The drone bot had already discovered him, entered the school without delay and caught him on the stairs, pinning him down in its grasp. It revealed a long, viciously sharp needle, and proceeded to strike Orion's neck.

Miraculously the needle hit the platinum cross hanging from Orion's necklace, and missed his skin.

"Ha! Would you look at that!"

The drone bot froze in confusion.

Orion snapped the needle in half, tearing the bot's hand from its socket, exposing frayed wires smoking and sparking in its place.

The drone fled.

The mother ship retreated.

"Ah! That's more like it!" Orion declared. *"Thank you Jesus!!"*

ABOUT THE AUTHOR

William "Enlightened Thug" Ewing

This is definitely a current picture of me and I have definitely not aged or gained weight since this photograph was taken.

FOLLOW US
ON FACEBOOK:
EXTRATERRESTRIAL
PUBLISHING HOUSE